Lone Bean

CHUDNEY ROSS

Lone Bean

Amistad
An Imprint of HarperCollinsPublishers

Amistad is an imprint of HarperCollins Publishers.

Lone Bean

www.harpercollinschildrens.com

Library of Congress Cataloging-in-Publication Data
Ross, Chudney.
Lone Bean / by Chudney Ross. — 1st ed.
p. cm.
Summary: Third grade starts off badly for eight-year-old Bean as she faces teasing from her two older sisters, learns that her former best friend wants nothing to do with her, and has to start taking music lessons.
ISBN 978-0-06-166011-5 (trade bdg.)
[1. Family life—Fiction. 2. Schools—Fiction. 3. Sisters—Fiction. 4. Best friends—Fiction. 5. Friendship—Fiction. 6. Violin—Fiction. 7. African Americans—Fiction.] I. Title.
PZ7.R19626Lon 2012 2011019973
[Fic]—dc22 CIP
AC

Typography by Michelle Gengaro-Kokmen
12 13 14 15 16 LP/RRDH 10 9 8 7 6 5 4 3 2 1
❖
First Edition

Dedicated to my mom—
I love you from here to the moon,
around the planets, and back

Contents

1
Call Me Bean

"Rise and shine. It's time to get ready for school." A voice rang in my ears.

I grabbed my glasses from the bedside table and pushed them up my nose. The blurry blob by the bedroom door transformed into my smiling daddy.

I hopped right up out of bed, but my sister Gardenia just grunted and hid her head under the covers. She is not a morning person.

"Up and at 'em," Dad said as he gave Gardenia's leg a shake. Then, with a quick turn, he headed down to Rose's room.

Rose is my oldest sister, and she is so lucky, because she gets her own room. I've always had to share mine with Gardenia. Mom said Rose needs her privacy because she's maturing into a young woman. No fair!

I'm the youngest of three girls and we're all named after flowers. Mom said she wanted her own bouquet, but I think she got a thorn bush with my sisters because they are m-e-a-n MEAN! I have a flower name too, of course, but it is long and hard to spell and terrible. I'll never tell anyone what it is. Mom and Dad sometimes call me by my real name when I'm in big trouble, but otherwise I'm just called Bean.

Today was the first day of school, and boy, was I excited. My new teacher was gonna be Ms. Sullivan. Rose had her in third grade and she said she was supernice. I was also excited because Carla was gonna be in my class.

Carla is my best friend. We've been friends forever and ever. Even when we weren't in the same class at school, we would help each other with our homework. We had sleepovers every weekend, and when she was really sick last year, I sat by her bed every day after school. I hadn't seen her all summer, and boy, did I miss her.

I headed down the hall to the bathroom, followed by a grouchy Gardenia, who had finally come out from under her covers. When I opened the bathroom door, steam fogged my glasses. Rose had been in the shower forever and was singing like she was Beyoncé, but she definitely didn't sound as good.

"Rose, would you shut up!" shouted Gardenia.

Rose just sang louder and off-key.

Gardenia growled and leaned her head into the sink to wash her face, just as I was about to spit out my toothpaste. Blue foamy paste exploded from my lips and slid down the side of her face.

"Gross!" She wiped her face with a washcloth. "Watch where you're spitting."

"Sorry," I said. Even though I tried to hold it in, I started to laugh. Luckily, Gardenia didn't clobber me. She laughed too.

"Breakfast time, ladies!" called Mom from downstairs.

We all finished getting ready and scurried downstairs, following the smell of bacon and oatmeal. I gave Mom a quick good-morning hug before I sat next to Dad at the table. Gardenia shoved pieces of bacon into her mouth before she even sat down. What a pig!

"Gardenia, please slow down," Dad said. "Put the food on your plate before you start gorging yourself."

Gardenia grabbed a handful of bacon, touched her plate with it, and then shoved it all into her mouth. Dad just sighed and shook his head.

The oatmeal looked delicious and sticky and gooey, so I shoved my finger way down deep in the bowl and circled it around.

"Bean—nasty! Get your grubby little finger out of there!" Rose bellowed, with her mouth so wide open, I could see her tonsils and that little ball dangling in the back of her throat.

"And I just saw her pick her nose," Gardenia joined in.

"I did not!" I glared at them with my angriest and meanest mad face. I pulled my finger out of the sticky oatmeal, popped it into my mouth, and crossed my eyes at my dumb sisters.

"Girls, that's enough," said Dad.

"Bean, please use a spoon," Mom said.

"Oh, all right," I said, and slid down low on the seat so only my eyes could be seen. I reached above my head to grab my spoon. I carefully scooped oatmeal and brought it down to where my mouth was. This kept me busy, so I didn't have to listen to Gardenia and Rose jabber on about summer camp.

"Remember on the high ropes course when Billy was belaying and your foot got caught?" Rose giggled.

"That was so embarrassing, and that harness hurt so bad." Gardenia laughed.

"Who is Billy and what is *belaying*?" I asked, but no one seemed to hear me.

I had no idea what they were talking about, because I hadn't gone to sleepaway camp with them. Mom and Dad said I was too young, so I had spent the summer at Grand Mommy's house with my cousin Tanya. We had so much fun playing in the sprinklers, drinking Slurpees, building forts, and riding bikes. And with no sisters around, it was the best summer ever!

"Okay, ladies, finish up your breakfast," Dad said. "Time to get a move on."

He kissed us each on the forehead—even Mom—and headed out the door to the college where he teaches. He's a music professor and can play almost any instrument, but he's best at piano and guitar. I can play piano, but not too good. "Chopsticks" is the only song I know.

"Have a great day, girls," Mom said. "I have to work late tonight, so I won't be home until after dinnertime. Be good for Daddy, okay?"

"Yes, Mom," we said all at the same time. I gave her a big hug.

Mom is an ob-gyn nurse at the hospital, which mean she helps deliver babies. She has to work long hours because you never know when a baby's gonna be born. I miss her when she has to work late, and I know Dad misses her too.

Mom handed me and Gardenia our lunch bags, then gave Rose some money, five whole dollars. She was starting middle school, so now she gets to buy lunch in the cafeteria. I wish I had some money instead of a stinky peanut-butter-and-jelly sandwich.

Just as I pulled on my backpack, Rose grabbed me by the hand and dragged me out the front door. She's in charge of making sure me and Gardenia get to school, but I didn't think that meant she had to rip my arm right off my body.

"Rose, you're breaking my fingers!" I scratched at the side of her hand.

"Stop being such a baby!" Rose barked, but she loosened her death grip, and we were on our way down the block.

I skipped and swung Rose's arm back and forth as we crossed Twenty-fifth Street. "Twenty-fourth . . . Twenty-third . . . Twenty-second. . . ." I counted out loud. It was fun to count backward, but the numbers stopped because we turned the corner onto Martin Luther King Jr. Boulevard.

I yelled, "Good morning, Martin Luther King Junior!"

He was a very important man. I had learned in second grade that he won the Nobel Peace Prize because he wanted blacks and whites to have equal rights.

"He had a dream, you know," I informed Rose.

Rose rolled her eyes at me and nearly yanked off my arm. She obviously didn't understand how important Martin Luther King is, so I pulled my hand out of her stinky, sweaty palm. I grabbed Gardenia's hand instead and swung it back and forth.

We turned the corner onto Coliseum Street, the street my school is on. Excited feelings swirled around in my tummy. We followed the fence around the playground and joined the crowds of kids and moms and dads filling the front of the building. I looked around, hoping to see some familiar faces, but there were too many big kids in the way. Mostly, all I saw were legs and feet. Gardenia ran off, with a wave over her shoulder, as Rose and I continued through the crowd.

"Come on, Bean," she said with a smile. "Let's go find Ms. Sullivan."

In the playground, all the kids were lining up. There was a big white circle painted on the cement with a green number 1 on it. *Eww!* I hate green. Green is for snakes and peas and boogers. Nasty! This was where the first grade lined up. I saw my old first-grade teacher, Ms. Ring. She was the nicest teacher ever. She taught me how to read, and we always played games to learn, instead of filling in worksheets from boring old workbooks. I ran over and gave her a quick hug.

"My goodness, Bean. Look how big you've gotten," she said as she gave me a warm hug back. Then she hugged Rose too. "And, Rose, aren't you in middle school now?"

Rose nodded and smiled.

"I remember when you were this big," Ms. Ring said as she put her hand right by my belly button. I looked up at Rose. I couldn't believe she was ever that small.

Me and Rose waved good-bye to Ms. Ring. We

passed the second graders and the big red painted number 2. Red used to be my favorite color, but now it just reminds me of my old second-grade teacher, Mr. Pane. Luckily, I didn't see him. I used to call him "Mr. Pain in the Neck."

"Mr. Pane's a pain in the neck. Mr. Pane's a pain in the neck!" I sang, but Rose covered my mouth with her sweaty hand. Yuck!

Finally, we marched up to the number 3. It was blue, which was perfect, because blue is my favorite color. Blue is like the sky and the ocean. I saw Ms. Sullivan, and even she was wearing blue. She was standing there in a pretty flowery dress and smiling big. I smiled even bigger.

"Hello, sweetheart," she said. "You must be Rose's little sister. What's your name?"

"My name is Bean and I'm eight and one-quarter years old." Ms. Sullivan nodded, so I continued, "I love to read and write and I'm really good at math."

Ms. Sullivan checked her clipboard and looked a bit confused.

"I don't see a Bean on my class list."

"Her real name is Chrysanthemum," Rose said, way too loud.

I told you my real name was terrible. I jabbed Rose in the side and quickly let Ms. Sullivan know what I like to be called. "But please call me Bean."

"Well, then, Bean, please go line up," she said.

I was glad she understood how very important it was to not call me Chrysanthemum. I dropped Rose's hand and wrapped my arms around Ms. Sullivan's middle. I liked her already.

"Bye, Rose," I said, and I gave her a squeeze around her middle too.

Even though I was annoyed that Rose told everyone my real name, she's my big sister and I love her.

2

A Not-So-Sweet Start to Third Grade

I marched right down the winding line behind Ms. Sullivan, and I saw some kids I knew.

John and Aisha gave me a wave, but that wasn't good enough for goody-two-shoes Gabrielle. She had to do this silly curtsy before she said, "Hello there, Bean. It is so very lovely to see you."

I just rolled my eyes and continued down the line. When I saw a boy I didn't know, I introduced myself. "Hello, my name is Bean." But before the boy could answer, a voice from the back of the line called, "No cuts!"

I ignored it, though, because I spotted my best friend!

"Carla!" I shouted.

She was wearing a green shirt, which was weird because we've always hated the color green, but I wrapped my arms around her anyway and gave her a big hug. She kinda hugged back, but not that big bear-hug kind that says "I'm so glad to see you." It was more like a loose, spaghetti-arms hug. Then she turned to Sam, the girl next to her, and started talking.

Sam's a tomboy and wears overalls and a baseball cap. She's okay, I guess, but we had never played with her before.

"Green apple Slurpees are so yummy." Carla licked her lips.

Wait! Did I just hear that right? I mean, green apple is disgusting! Me and Carla's favorite flavor at 7-Eleven had always been blue raspberry.

"It was so funny when you got that brain freeze and fell on the floor right there in the store." Sam laughed and mimicked what I guess Carla looked like rolling around and holding her head.

"How was your summer, Carla?" I said, jumping in and trying to get her attention.

"We had so much fun," she said as she linked arms with Sam.

"Hey, you!" the voice called again from the back of the line. I ignored it again because I was trying to figure out what was going on here.

"I thought we were best friends, Carla."

"We were," Carla said in a serious voice. "But best friends return phone calls and emails."

"I tried to write back, but Grand Mommy's computer is so slow and it took so long to load. I . . . um . . . guess my emails never went through. I got your message, though, and I called you back when I got home, but it was busy and . . . um went to voicemail. I didn't leave a message because I thought I would just call again, but I . . . um . . . never got the chance to. . . . I guess I got caught up in all the fun with Tanya. You know, I really didn't mean to be a bad friend over the summer." I rambled on and on.

"I said *no cuts*!" the voice sounded really angry this time.

I spun around to see who it was. It was Terrible Tanisha, the class bully. Last year, she sat behind me and blew spitballs. One time, she stuck a big wad of gum in my hair and I had to cut out a huge chunk. She is nasty and mean and just terrible!

"You better get to the back of the line or I'll clobber you!" Tanisha yelled with her fist in the air.

"Fine," I said. Carla and Sam went back to talking to each other, and I marched to the very end of the line, all alone.

"Loser," Tanisha said with a laugh as I passed her.

The class started moving. I dragged my feet, trailing behind. I followed as the line wove in and out of the other groups of kids and up to the main building. Carla was holding the big red door for everyone.

I was about to try and talk to her again, but—*slam!* She shut the door right before I got through. Oh . . . that was cold!

I pushed open the heavy door and stomped the rest of the way to Room Three, where all the kids were rushing around, trying to find which desk had their name tag on it. I always like to sit right up front, but when I checked the first row of desks, I didn't see my name. There had to be some mistake! All the seats were already filled by Jerry, John, Aisha, Carla, and Sam.

"Aisha, I'm so glad you're sitting next to me," said Carla with a big cheesy grin. Carla doesn't even like Aisha. She once said Aisha was dumb as a rock.

I didn't have time to feel bad for myself, though. I had to find my seat. I finally spotted my name tag in the fourth row. It wasn't so bad, because it was right by the window, where you could see the whole playground. I put my bag down, but just as I started to sit, Terrible Tanisha slid her big, fat butt into the chair and—*bang!* She knocked me and my name tag right on the floor. *Ouch!*

"Ms. Sullivan!" I yelped.

"What's the problem, ladies?" Ms. Sullivan asked calmly as she walked over. She must not have realized the seriousness of this situation.

"Tanisha just stole my seat."

"Did not! My name was on this desk!" Tanisha shouted, waving her name tag above her head.

"Was not!"

"Girls, there are plenty of seats for everyone. Bean, why don't you take one of those empty seats in the back?"

"But this one was mine."

"Sorry, sweetheart," Ms. Sullivan said. She turned and headed back to the front of the room. Maybe Ms. Sullivan wasn't so nice after all.

"Tattletale," whispered Tanisha under her breath as I turned around to look for another seat.

"You can have mine," Stanley said.

I was about to say no, because Stanley is stinky. He might seriously be the smelliest kid in all of California. But then I realized it was right behind Carla.

"Thanks, Stanley," I said, and I held my breath.

I slid into my perfect new seat. Carla turned to see what was going on, but then, without even a little trace of a smile, she whipped back around.

"Okay, everyone, we are going to start this

morning with a 'get to know you' activity," said Ms. Sullivan. "Everyone will choose a partner, and you will interview each other. Then each pair will come up to the front of the room and share what they've learned."

I started wiggling in my seat, waiting for the okay from Ms. Sullivan to choose a partner. I needed to be with Carla. I mean, I had to keep trying to make her my friend again.

"Okay, find a partner, but try to pick someone you don't know very well," Ms. Sullivan said. Then, just like at the start of a race, everyone rushed around the room.

I reached out and tapped Carla's shoulder. "Wanna be partners?" I asked, and smiled my biggest, happiest, please-pick-me smile.

"Sorry, Sam and I are already partners," Carla sneered. She pulled her chair close to Sam's.

"But . . . you guys already know each other."

Carla rolled her eyes and said, "So do we, Bean."

I looked around for another partner. Aisha and Gabrielle were already sitting together by the window. Joshua and John were on the floor in the back. Renee and a new girl were huddled in the library corner. It looked like everyone already had a partner. But then I spotted Jerry sitting alone.

"Jerry! Jerry!" I yelled as I ran toward him, waving my arms in the air to get his attention.

"Sorry, Bean. I'm already partners with Mark," he said before I even reached his desk.

"Mark? Who is Mark?" I said frantically. "I don't see a Mark."

"He's new and he's in the bathroom."

I started to panic. Stinky Stanley was looking at me with puppy-dog eyes from the back of the room. It was nice of him to give me his seat and all, but I didn't want to be his partner now. I wasn't sure I could stand the smell.

Next, I spotted Terrible Tanisha. She obviously didn't have a partner yet because she is m-e-a-n MEAN! I flipped my eyes back and forth. Stanley or Tanisha? Tanisha or Stanley? What kind of choice is that?

I grabbed my notebook and quickly headed over

to Stanley, held my breath, and mouthed the words, *Wanna be my partner?*

He nodded his head yes a million times.

When Ms. Sullivan saw that Tanisha was all alone, she forced Aisha and Gabrielle to work with her as a threesome. I could tell they were not happy about it at all.

I was not excited to be partners with Stanley either, but at least he was better than Terrible Tanisha.

"Here are some questions to get you started," Ms. Sullivan said as she wrote on the chalkboard.

Name and birthday
Does your partner have brothers and sisters?
What did your partner do for summer vacation?
Favorite color, food, sport
What does your partner want to be when he/she grows up?

"But feel free to ask and explore whatever seems interesting about your partner. You have the next fifteen minutes to interview each other," Ms. Sullivan said. "I'll be coming around to see if you need any help."

I pulled my chair up to Stanley's, but not too close. He smelled like tuna fish mixed with pickle juice and spinach that had sat in the sun on a super-hot day. *Eww.*

I cleared my throat and tried to sit up straight like one of those interviewers on TV.

"Let's get started. Stanley, when is your birthday?"

"January nineteenth. When is yours?"

"No. I ask the questions," I told him. "You go after."

"Sorry," he said, and I got back to the interview.

I imagined the TV studio lights shining down on us as we sat on the sofa of my very own TV show, called *Bean Time!*

"Hello, Stanley," I started. "Thank you so much for taking time out of your busy schedule to give us this exclusive interview."

"What does *exclusive* mean?" Stanley asked. He looked back at me blankly, but I just continued because this was *my* TV show. "Tell me about your family. Do you have a mom and a dad?"

"Yes," he answered.

"Any brothers or sisters?"

"Nope," said Stanley with a shake of his head.

"Really? No fair! I have two and they are so annoying," I said as I made a note in my notebook. Then I continued, "How was your summer vacation?"

"Good."

Ms. Sullivan walked by just then, and said, "Stanley, try to answer with more than one word."

I was a little annoyed that she was interrupting my TV show, but I let it go because she's the boss of the classroom, you know.

"My summer was good," Stanley said. Then he added, "I went to Disneyland and—"

"Awesome," I interrupted. "What else?"

"I went to my grandma's house."

"Me too!" I shouted.

"Did you have fun?" Stanley asked.

"I told you not to ask questions," I reminded him.

"What's your favorite color and food and sport?"

"Well, I guess my favorite color is green."

"Ugh!" I scrunched up my nose. "I hate green."

"I also like blue."

"That's better," I said, and made some more notes in my notebook.

"And I like carrots and pretzels and ice cream," Stanley continued.

"Yuck, double yuck . . . and yummy," I responded. "And?"

"And what?" he asked.

"What's your favorite sport?" I said, without even checking the board.

"I don't really play sports." He shrugged his shoulders.

"You don't?"

"Nope. Not really, but I can play the saxophone. I want to be a famous musician when I grow up."

The saxophone is a cool instrument. I listened to a supergood guy named John Coltrane play the saxophone on one of Dad's CDs. I couldn't imagine Stanley ever being as cool as him.

"Okay. Time to switch interviewers," Ms. Sullivan called from the front of the room.

"Umm . . . ," Stanley mumbled, and peeked at the questions on the chalkboard. "What is your—"

"Hold it!" I said, stopping him. I already knew all the questions, so I gave him all the info at once. "My name is Bean Gibson. I am eight and a quarter and my birthday is June fifth. I have a mom and dad and two annoying sisters. Well, Rose isn't terrible, but you know. I had a superfun summer because, while my sisters where at sleepaway camp, I got to go to my grand mommy's house and spend the whole summer playing with Tanya. She's my cousin, but she is also my best friend . . . now. My favorite color is blue. I h-a-t-e HATE the color green. My favorite foods are blue raspberry Slurpees and Cheetos and pasta. I hate pickles and tuna. I like running fast and riding my bike."

Stanley's pen was scribbling a zillion miles a minute. I stopped so he could catch up.

"Did you get all that?" I asked.

"Almost."

"Well, how much did you get?"

"Um . . . your name and your birthday."

"Good grief," I said, and then I repeated everything again, real slow.

"Um, Bean? Can I at least ask one of the questions?"

"Fine. What's left?"

"Um. What do you want to be when you grow up?"

"Hmm . . . I don't really know. Maybe a fireman . . . I mean firewoman. Maybe a nurse, like my mom. Maybe an astronaut."

"Okay, time's up. Everyone back to your seats," Ms. Sullivan called from the front of the room.

3

If You Don't Have Something Nice to Say . . .

"Who would like to share first?" Ms. Sullivan asked the class.

Everyone's hands shot up. Of course she chose Carla and Sam because they were sitting right up front. No fair!

Sam started. "This is Carla. Her birthday is December twenty-second. She has a mom and an older sister. This summer, she went to visit her grandparents in Mexico, but she spent most of the summer here with me. We rode bikes and went to the swimming pool and made a secret club."

I sank down deep into my chair and tried not to listen.

"Her favorite color is green and her favorite foods are spaghetti and green apple Slurpees."

I couldn't help it. My mouth opened and out flew, "No, it's not!"

"Yes, it is . . . now!" Carla shouted back.

"Bean, please stay quiet till it's your turn," Ms. Sullivan said.

"When she grows up, Carla wants to be a teacher," said Sam, finishing up.

Everyone clapped, except for me, of course. Instead, I put my hands over my face to stop my mouth from letting everyone know that Carla really wants to be a nurse when she grows up, just like my mom.

"Carla, your turn to tell us about Sam," Ms. Sullivan said.

"This is Sam and she's my best friend," Carla said.

I covered my ears with my hands so I wouldn't have to hear the rest. Carla and Sam giggled and danced around in the front of the room for what seemed like forever. Aisha, Gabrielle, and Tanisha went next, but I couldn't even listen because I was too upset. Mark and Jerry went after them.

And then it was our turn. Me and Stanley walked up to the front of the room.

"You go first," I told Stanley. He looked nervous, so I gave him a little shove.

"This is Bean. Her birthday is June fifth." As he spoke, I put my hands over my head and spun around so everyone could get a good look at me.

"Her favorite color is blue. She hates green. Her favorite food is blue raspberry Slurpees. She hates pickles."

"And tuna," I said as I scrunched up my nose and stuck out my tongue for extra effect.

"She has a mom and a dad and two sisters. She had a great summer at her grandmother's house playing with her cousin, I mean, best friend, Tanya."

I turned to see Carla's reaction, but she wasn't even looking at me. She was passing a folded-up note to Sam.

"And when I grow up, I'm going to have my own TV show," I added and took a bow, followed by a curtsy.

Everyone clapped, even Carla, but I could tell she didn't mean it.

"Hello, everyone," I said in my best TV-show-host voice. "This is Stanley. His birthday is in January. He's lucky because he doesn't have any brothers or sisters. He's even luckier because he went to Disneyland this summer. Also, he can play the saxophone, which is a supercool instrument."

"Bean and Stanley sittin' in a tree k-i-s-s-i-n-g," Sam sang under her breath. I knew Ms. Sullivan couldn't hear from the back of the room, where she was watching the presentations.

Carla laughed, and so did the other kids sitting around them. My cheeks turned beet red and I wanted to run out of the room. I didn't want everyone to think I liked Stanley, so I said, "He smells like rotten tuna fish, so don't get too close." I pretended to gag and I held my nose. Everyone laughed, and I walked back to my seat, leaving Stanley alone and sad in the front of the room.

"Bean, that was not nice," Ms. Sullivan bellowed as she marched toward me. "I think you owe Stanley an apology."

She was glaring down at me like an ogre, so I had no other choice but to do what she said.

"Sorry, Stanley," I said without even turning around. I felt bad that I had hurt his feelings, but I had no other choice, you know.

"If you don't have something nice to say, then don't say anything at all," Ms. Sullivan told me sternly.

When the presentations were all done, Ms. Sullivan went over the class rules. The last one was "Treat everyone with respect." I thought that one was probably especially for me.

The rest of the day was pretty terrible. I sat alone at lunch and ate my peanut-butter-and-jelly sandwich, which had gotten all smushed when I sat on my backpack by accident. And during recess, I didn't have anyone to play with, so I threw rocks at the fence, which was no fun at all.

After recess, we marched back to the classroom and the bad day just kept getting worse. I usually l-o-v-e LOVE reading, but this time I couldn't follow along. Carla and I always used to trace the lines of the book with our fingers. But now I had to share a book with goody-two-shoes Gabrielle, and every time I traced the lines, she kept swatting my finger away like a fly. Then, in math, which is usually easy-peasy, my numbers kept getting all jumbled up because Carla was whispering and passing notes to Sam.

Brrrrr-i-ing! The bell finally rang. I jumped right up out of my seat and was the first one to the door. It took forever to get everyone lined up, but finally we made it out of the room, down the hall, and out to the playground.

I waved good-bye to Ms. Sullivan with a smile, but then I spotted Carla and Sam skipping toward the gate. Carla always used to walk home with me and my sisters.

I stood slumped over in the middle of the playground, remembering all the fun me and Carla used to have after school. I snapped back to the real world when Rose found me and asked, "So, how was the first day?"

"Bad."

Before I could explain why, Rose spotted Gardenia coming out of the building and yanked me in her direction.

We headed out on Coliseum Street, and when we hit Twenty-fifth Street, I raced ahead. I wanted to get to the computer first, so I could email Tanya. Without thinking, I jumped off the curb into the street.

"Bean, get over here. You know you can't cross the street alone," Rose said as she caught up to me.

Gardenia's lucky and can cross the street all by herself. She looked both ways, crossed, and passed me and Rose right by. Now there was no way I was going to get to the computer first.

When I spotted the house, I ran as fast as I could, but I was still behind Gardenia when we burst through the back door.

"Whoa, there, ladies," Dad said, startled. "Slow down. I want to hear about your first day."

"It was good," Gardenia said. Then she headed straight to the snack drawer and grabbed the last fruit roll-up.

"I'll tell you all about it later, Dad!" Rose yelled over her shoulder as she headed straight upstairs. "I gotta use the bathroom!"

"How about you, Bean?" asked Dad.

"Oh, fine . . . super . . . fantastic," I said, giving Dad a fake smile.

I couldn't believe my luck. The computer was still free. I threw my backpack on the floor and plopped myself down.

You've got mail, the computer said.

I scanned the mail and it was all junk, so I opened up a new message box and typed in Tanya's email address. Rose walked by to go play outside, while I sat and thought about what to say. Then my fingers started typing.

To: TTBaby@mailman.com

From: LilBean@mailman.com

Subject: Hows it goin?

Hey Tanya--

3rd grade is bad. My girl Carla has a new best frend and now I got no one 2 play with.

I miss u soooo much! Wish u went 2 the same skool as me.

How r u?

Bean :-)

"Dad, Bean's hogging the computer again!" Gardenia glared as she pushed through the door from the kitchen. "She's taking forever."

"Am not!"

"Bean, give Gardenia a turn on the computer," Dad said, taking her side, of course. "I want to have a little chat with you anyway."

I followed Dad into the kitchen and plopped down at the table.

"Well, honey, now that you are a big third grader," he said as he sat down next to me, "it's time to start taking piano lessons."

"But I don't want to play the piano," I protested.

"Why not?"

"Because Rose plays the piano."

And Rose plays the piano really well. She can play Mozart and Beethoven and even some songs you hear on the radio. Gardenia plays the flute, and when she plays, she sounds like a songbird.

"You'll be great."

"But Rose said my fingers are too short and nubby."

"She was just teasing you. Your fingers are perfect," said Dad as he tapped my hand with his. "And your sister plays so well because she takes lessons and practices. Like I always say—"

"I know. I know," I said. I'd heard Dad say it a million times. "Practice makes perfect. But I still don't want to play the piano."

"Bean, it's time to start taking music lessons, so it's either the piano or another instrument, but you have to choose one ASAP."

"Fine," I said. I crossed my arms.

"What's going on with you, Bean?" Dad put his arm around my shoulder. "You don't seem like your happy self."

And I didn't feel like my happy self, either. I let out a loud sigh and dropped my head to the cool table.

"What's up? You can talk to me."

"Carla has a new best friend. I don't think Ms. Sullivan likes me, and now I have to play an instrument." Tears started filling up my eyes. "Third grade is terrible."

Dad snuggled me in close to him. "It's just the first day of school. And you know what? Music always makes me feel better when I am feeling blue."

I hoped he was right, but for now my mind was spinning with Carla and Ms. Sullivan and musical instruments. It all made me feel dizzy and sick, so I went outside to get some fresh air.

Rose and her friend Gina were playing hopscotch on the driveway. They'd drawn the squares with pretty pink and purple chalk.

"Can I play?" I called out.

"We've already started, Bean. Sorry," Rose said as she threw the stone to the number 6 and hopped, jumped, hopped, jumped all the way to it.

Gardenia burst out of the door and shoved right past me. I glared at her as she joined Rose and Gina—who immediately let her play with them. I decided I didn't even want to play with my stupid-head sisters anyway.

4

One Is Silver and the Other's Gold

You've got mail, the computer said.

I clicked on the mailbox and *yes!* There was an email from Tanya.

To: LilBean@mailman.com

From: TTBaby@mailman.com

Subject: Re: Hows it goin?

Hey Bean,

Miss u 2. Sorry u had a bad day. Mine was great. My teacher is so nice. GTG cause my friend Donna is over. TTYL!

T

Tanya had a friend to play with and I was all alone.

I heard Mom come in the back door.

"Hey, honey," said Dad.

"I'm exhausted." Mom sighed.

"Go relax. I'll get started on dinner."

"Oh, it's okay," she said. "I know you have lessons tonight. I'm on dinner."

"Thanks. I'll put the water on to boil for the spaghetti while you change."

Mom came into the living room and took off her jacket. She was wearing blue scrubs, which kinda look like pajamas. She wears them every day to work at the hospital. They look so comfy, and she is so lucky that she never has to worry about what to wear or if it's gonna match.

“Hey, there, Bean. What are you doing?” asked Mom.

“Just checking my email.”

“How was the first day?” she said, spinning my chair around.

I couldn’t even get a word out before my eyes filled up and I started to cry. I fell into Mom’s arms, and she held me tight.

“Third grade is terrible. I hate it and I’m never going back.”

“How come? What happened?” Mom led me to the couch.

We snuggled into the cushions. I said, “Carla has a new friend and they don’t want to play with me and they keep laughing and passing notes in the front row, so I can’t concentrate, and Gabrielle wouldn’t let me follow along in the book with my finger like Carla always does.” I gasped to catch my breath between sobs. “And I had to be partners with Stanley and he’s smelly and people laughed because Sam said I like him and Ms. Sullivan got mad at me and now Dad is telling me I have to play the dumb piano.”

"Oh, baby," Mom said as she hugged me tighter. "You had quite a day."

I mopped up my tears with my wet sleeve and said, "I hate third grade."

"Bean, third grade will all get better, I promise. It was just the first day. Sometimes a new year takes some getting used to. And baby, you and Carla have been friends for so long. This will work itself out."

Work itself out? But *how*?

"And, Bean, don't listen to what other people say. If you like Stanley, that's just fine."

"I don't like Stanley," I said with my most very serious tone of voice.

"All right then, but remember, it's important to treat people the way you would like to be treated. Okay?"

I do not like to be called names, so I felt bad that I had called Stanley *stinky* today.

"Do you have homework?" asked Mom.

"A little."

"Then get to work. It's almost time for dinner," she said, and then she disappeared up the stairs to change her clothes. If I got to wear blue scrubs like Mom, I would never take them off. I would wear them to bed and to school and even to parties.

I grabbed my backpack and set up at the kitchen table. I had one sheet of math and the letters *A* and *B* in my cursive writing book, and I had to write my spelling words in sentences. I decided to work on the cursive writing first. Uppercase *A*'s are kinda hard, but I got into a groove with the lowercase ones. Just as I was starting to trace the uppercase *B*'s . . .

Knock! Knock! Someone was at the door. I tried to ignore it and keep making my letters, but whoever it was kept pounding and pounding.

"Can you get that, Bean?" Mom asked.

I got up with a huff and pulled my chair over to the door. You have to look out the peephole before you open up, you know. I could only see the top of someone's head. It kinda looked like a head I knew, but it couldn't be. Could it? I moved the chair away and swung open the door. No way! Stinky Stanley was right there at my back door.

"Hi, Bean," he said.

"What are you doing here?" I gasped as a whiff of yuck filled my nose.

"Hey, Stanley," Dad said as he came in from the living room. "Ready to get started?"

I turned to Dad and asked, "Started on what?"

"I'm working with Stanley on his saxophone. He has quite a musical talent."

I stood there with my mouth so wide open that a bird could have flown in. They walked right by me and into the living room, where they set up by the piano. I couldn't believe Stinky Stanley was in my living room and now my poor ears would have to listen to his terrible saxophone playing.

They started to play, and boy, was I surprised! Stanley was not bad at all. He was actually super-duper good. He sounded almost like they do on Dad's jazz CDs. I tried to get back to my homework, but all that bebopping in the living room was very distracting.

I finally finished my cursive writing and started to smell dinner. Mmm . . . spaghetti and meat-balls . . . and garlic bread. I worked on my spelling, then started on my math. It was easy as pie. Mmm . . . pie would be yummy too! My stomach gurgled. I was starving. I counted the time till dinner. One meatball, two meatballs, three meatballs, four . . .

"Would you like to stay for dinner?" Dad asked Stanley when they came into the kitchen. I held my breath and shut my eyes. No. Say no, Stanley! *Say no!*

"No, thanks, Mr. Gibson. I've gotta get home," he said. "Bye, Bean. See you tomorrow at school."

"Bye," I said with a big smile, and this one was a real one because I was happy he couldn't stay.

At dinner, my sisters jabbered on about how great their first day of school was. Gardenia was excited because her best friend, Whitney, is in her class and some boy named Kevin who she l-o-v-e LOVES! Rose kept going on about how, in middle school, you get your own locker in the hallway and go to different classrooms with different teachers for every subject. Sounded like a pain to me, but I couldn't even get a word in edgewise.

"How was your day?" Dad asked Mom, and

finally my sisters shut their mouths.

"Oh, my goodness, it was a busy one. It felt like a never-ending flood of babies," Mom said with a laugh. "Five in all."

"Wow! That's a lot of birthdays in one day," I said.

"Bean, did you tell Mommy about your day?" Dad asked.

"Yep," I said as I sulked down deep in my chair. I felt so sad that I wasn't even hungry anymore.

"You and Carla will work it out," Rose said. She patted my leg under the table.

Mom said the same thing, but I wish someone would tell me how.

"And till then, I'm sure Stanley could be a good friend," Mom suggested.

"No way!" I shouted. "Are you kidding me?"

"Bean"—Dad looked me straight in the eyes—"Stanley is a very nice boy."

"But I want to be friends with Carla."

"There is nothing wrong with making new friends," Mom said.

"That's right," Dad agreed. "It's just like that song we used to sing when you were little. 'Make new friends, but keep the old. One is silver and the other's gold.'"

"Whatever." I groaned.

Dad got up from the table and put his plate in the sink, followed by Rose and Gardenia.

"Grab your instruments, girls—let's make some music," Dad sang.

They always practiced at night before bed. I knew soon I would have to play with them too . . . once I figured out which instrument was better than the piano.

"Bean, up to your room to wash up," said Mom. "It's almost bedtime for you."

I hate that I have to go to bed before everyone else just 'cause I'm the youngest, but I marched myself up the stairs anyway. I brushed my teeth, washed my face, and put on my pajamas. I grabbed my book, *Ramona Quimby, Age 8,* and climbed into bed. I love the Ramona books because she is funny and gets into trouble a lot and also because we are the very same age, you know. But tonight I couldn't concentrate because there was too much going on inside my brain.

I could hear a muffled Rose playing the piano and a garbled Gardenia on the flute. Usually, the music lulls me to sleep, but not tonight. I stared at the ceiling fan as it turned and turned and turned. Luckily, Mom stuck her head in the door just as I was starting to get d-i-z-z-y DIZZZZZZY!

"Good night, Bean," she said. She turned out the lights and closed the door, but she left it open just a crack, so it wouldn't be too dark.

5

The Missing Link

Every day after school, I ran straight to the computer, but not today. When I slid through the door, Dad was waiting in the kitchen.

"So?" he said.

So what? I racked my brain. I had been a good girl the whole first week of school, doing my homework each night without complaining and getting along with my sisters.

"Have you decided which instrument you want to play?" Dad asked with a smile. "Today is the day!"

"Ah," I sighed. I wasn't in trouble after all. I still hadn't thought about which instrument to play, but I knew for sure it wasn't gonna be the piano or the flute. I racked my brain some more for something cool and different and special . . . something like me!

Dad drummed his fingers on the table while he waited for my answer.

"I got it!" I shouted. "The cello! I wanna play the cello!"

"The cello?" Dad repeated with a wrinkled brow. "Why the cello?"

"Because it's b-i-g BIG and cool, and no one else plays it."

"Okay, if that's what you want," Dad said as he shook his head. "Follow me. We'll find you one in the garage."

I trailed right behind him out the back door, down the steps, and around the side of the house. We stepped into the dark and spooky garage, and a shiver ran down my spine as Dad swatted away a spiderweb. *Eww.*

There are no cars in our garage. Only spooks and

spiders and oh, yeah . . . that's where Dad keeps all sorts of instruments. He went to the far-back dark corner and pulled out a huge—and I mean really huge—leather case. It was skinny at the top and really fat at the bottom and very, very dusty.

"Here you go, Bean. This cello is all yours," he said. He leaned the huge case on my shoulder.

Ugh! It was even heavier than it looked. I tugged and pulled and finally got it just right and ready to drag into the house. I heaved and pulled, but my back felt like it was gonna crack for sure.

"Dad, can you help me carry it?" I asked as I huffed and puffed and pushed and pulled.

"First lesson is that the cello is heavy, and if you are going to play it, you're going to have to carry it," he said.

"But—"

"But nothing, baby."

And with that, he left me in the dark garage alone with the biggest, stupidest cello ever. Maybe if I was a big, muscly weightlifter, I could have played the cello, but since I'm not, I searched the garage for something a little more my size. The trombone? Nope. I didn't want my cheeks all stretched and puffed. The drums? No way. They are even bigger and heavier that the cello.

Then I saw it in the corner off by itself. The violin! That was it. It's a string instrument and you play it with a bow, just like the cello, only it's way, way smaller. I grabbed the case, easy as pie, and ran back into the house to let Dad know.

"Dad, I wanna play the violin instead," I said, showing him the case proudly.

"What happened to the cello?"

"I changed my mind, but I won't change it again. I love, love, love the violin."

I gave the dusty leather case a hug to show how much I really did love it.

"Okay, then, the violin it is."

I headed into the living room to get to work on my homework. I plopped myself down on the floor by the coffee table just as Mom came in.

"Hello, honey," she said, greeting Dad with a big hug. Then she stuck her head into the living room and blew kisses to me and my sisters. "And kisses for my favorite flowers in the whole world!" she sang.

Mom took over for Dad, cooking in the kitchen so he could come make sure everyone was doing their homework.

"I'm already done," said Gardenia. She danced around the living room.

"I'm working on it," I grumbled as I tried to focus on my spelling words.

"Nice work, ladies." Dad turned his attention to Gardenia. "Pull out your flute and let's make some music."

She grabbed her case and put her flute together piece by piece. Rose came downstairs and sat at the piano, ready to play. But before they could get started, Dad said, "Your sister is going to learn how to play the violin."

"Really? That's cool, Bean," Rose said.

"Once Bean gets going, you guys can all play together." Dad beamed. "We'll have the Gibson Family Trio!"

Dad used to play in an orchestra in college and

a rock band too. Since he has no time to rock with his old band, he's always been excited about making a new band here at home. I've been the missing link, you know.

"No way, Dad! I'm going to be a solo artist, and I am definitely not gonna play with Bean," said Gardenia—as if I wasn't even in the room. "She doesn't know how."

"She's going to learn," Dad said.

"Yeah! And I'll be better than you!" I stuck my tongue out at her.

"I doubt it." She laughed.

"Guess what?" Dad said. "My students are putting on a big holiday musical performance at the college. And I would like all of you to play in the show."

"Not me, though. Right?" I asked nervously.

"Yes, ma'am! You too," Dad said.

"But I don't even know how to play."

"We'll have all of Thanksgiving break to practice, and you'll play something simple. Don't worry, sweetheart. This is gonna be fun."

Gardenia practiced with Dad while I did my homework. She may be rotten, but she sounded beautiful. There was no way I would be that good by Christmas.

I finished my homework just as Gardenia finished her lesson. Then it was Rose's turn. She sat up really straight and started playing. She can play with both hands at once and with all her fingers moving at the same time. She was gonna be the star of the holiday performance, for sure.

I lay on the floor listening to Rose play. She was even better than Gardenia. My stomach twisted and turned into knots. What if the violin was too hard?

Rose finished her lesson, and Dad gave her a high five. "Nice job, Rose!"

"Practice makes perfect," Rose said with a giggle. She hopped up from the piano. "Your turn, Bean."

I got up slowly and brought my violin case over to Dad. My hands shook and my fingers felt like Jell-O as I unlatched the buckles and opened the case. I pulled out the shiny wooden violin and the long matching bow. Dad twisted and turned the knobs at the top till the strings were tight. Then he showed me how to hold the violin between my chin and my left shoulder. He also showed me where to put my left fingers on the strings, in what he called "open position." Then he showed me how to hold the bow in my other hand.

"Now let's try to make a sound," Dad said.

He showed me how to pull the bow across one string at a time. I did it just the way Dad showed me, but . . . *screeeeeech!*

I scrunched up my nose at the awful sound and Gardenia covered her ears. But not Dad. He smiled and seemed to enjoy it.

"Good job, Bean," he said.

"What? That sounded terrible."

"We've got to start somewhere," said Dad, "and that was nice and loud."

"Sure was," Gardenia said, scrunching up her nose.

I slid the bow across the strings again and again, but each time I pulled the bow, it sounded worse than the last. Like, really terrible!

"Press a little harder on the strings and pull the bow slowly."

I kept trying and it got a little better, but it was still b-a-d BAD!

"Now, let's try to make a G," Dad suggested.

He was talking about musical notes, you know. Dad showed me which string to pull the bow on.

I did it just like he showed me and . . . *screeeeeeeeech!*

"I can't do this!"

"It's going to take some time to get the hang of it," Dad said. "Try again."

I tried and tried, till my back hurt from sitting up so straight. My arms ached from holding the violin and the bow in the air.

"Dad, I need a break," I said. I shook my arms out and stretched my back. "This violin is hard work."

Dad made me try a couple more times before agreeing to give me a rest.

"You did well for the first day," he said, giving me a high five. Then he headed to the kitchen to keep Mom company while she made dinner.

Gardenia sat at the computer and said, "You are horrible."

"I know," I said as I put the violin and bow back in their leather case.

"You're gonna get booed right off that stage at the holiday performance."

I put my violin case away and collapsed on the couch. Mom told me once that if you think about something going good in your head, it'll work itself out in real life. I decided to try. As I lay there, I imagined standing in front of crowds and crowds of people. A spotlight came on and circled me as I stood in a pretty dress with my violin in my hand. The audience stared in anticipation as I got ready to play. I took a deep breath and . . . *screeeech!* My violin made the most terrible, awful, dreadful sound, and everyone howled with laughter.

"Dinnertime!" Mom called.

Thank goodness.

I trudged into the kitchen and plopped myself down at the table. Mom had made mac and cheese, one of my favorites! Even though I was still upset about the silly violin, that didn't stop me from shoveling spoonful after spoonful into my mouth. Yum!

After dinner, I headed upstairs to get ready for bed. I brushed my teeth, washed my face, and put on my pajamas. Instead of taking out my book, I pulled out the violin case from under my bed. I decided to give this stinkin' violin one more try. Mom, Dad, Rose, and Gardenia were still downstairs, so no one would hear.

I took the violin out of the case and placed it on my shoulder. I held the neck of the violin gently, with my fingers curved over the strings, just like Dad had shown me. Then I took out the bow, placed it on the second string, and slid. *Screeeech!*

I felt like I was gonna cry, but I fought to hold the tears in. I really wanted to get this. I kept trying again and again, but it kept screeching and screeching. Then, all of a sudden, to my surprise, one steady, in-tune note sang from the string.

It wasn't a song or anything, but it was a start . . . a good start. I climbed into bed still smiling, but just as I snuggled under the covers, my bedroom door opened with a creak.

"Bean?" Gardenia whispered.

"What?"

"*Screeeeeeeeeeeech!*" she wailed. And she ran back down the stairs, laughing hysterically.

6

Goody, Goody Gumdrops

For Halloween, our class was allowed to put on our costumes during recess. I was a rock star. Mom had bought me the most beautiful sequined dress from the thrift store. Dad let me borrow a microphone from the garage, and Rose gave me some sparkly makeup.

When I got all dressed up and fluffed out my hair, I looked awesome. But no one told me how great my costume was and no one wanted to watch me put on a concert . . . except for Stanley, but he doesn't count because I didn't even want him to.

When you don't have a best friend, there is no one to stand in line with and no one to sit with at lunch and no one to talk to and no one to trade your carrots or milk with. And worst of all, no one to play with at recess, so I just plopped down on the bench and watched everyone run around in their costumes.

Some days, though, I would go to the principal's office at recess. Not because I was in trouble or anything, but because I liked to spend time with Ms. Gloria, the secretary.

Ms. Gloria sits at a big oak desk and answers the phones while she files her long pink-painted nails. She's really pretty and she wears red lipstick.

"Hey, Ms. Gloria," I said as I poked my head into the office.

"Hi there, honey." Ms. Gloria greeted me with a warm smile and the usual question. "Are things any better with Carla?"

I always tell Ms. Gloria what's going on. "She totally hates me."

"Oh, Bean, I'm sure she doesn't."

"Need any help today?" I asked, changing the subject.

I crossed my fingers behind my back because I hoped she had an errand for me to run. My favorite is when she lets me go in the teachers' lounge to copy papers for her. No kids are allowed in the teachers' lounge, except me when I'm on official office business.

"I've got some mail to deliver to Room Four," she said.

"I'll make it a speedy delivery."

I took the envelope and spun around to head into the hall. Standing in the doorway was goody-two-shoes Gabrielle.

Gabrielle is the most polite person I have ever met and she never gets in trouble. Also, she is always dressed like she's going to a party. She wears dresses with matching hair bows. I don't think it feels very comfortable, but she sure does look nice all the time. I only have one fancy dress like that, but it's for church. I usually just wear jeans and a T-shirt.

"Hello, Ms. Gloria," she said in her sweet-as-sugar

voice. "I just wanted to stop by to see how you are doing today and see if maybe you might need help with anything."

No way! This girl was trying to take my job!

"Oh, you girls are so nice," Ms. Gloria said with a smile. "Bean is going to deliver some mail for me. Why don't you go with her and make sure it gets to Room Four safe and sound?"

"Goody, goody gumdrops!" she sang.

"I can handle it," I said quickly. "You don't need to come with me."

"No worries at all," said Gabrielle. "I would love to accompany you."

I held the envelope tight in my hand as I rushed into the hall, with Gabrielle tailing close behind.

"I love to help Ms. Gloria," Gabrielle said as she clip-clopped like a horse to catch up to me. "Don't you?"

I didn't say anything. I just kept walking because I was on a mission. I opened the door to Room Four and handed the envelope to Ms. Charles, the other third-grade teacher.

"Thank you, girls."

"No problem," I said.

"Our pleasure," Gabrielle chimed in. "And don't you look nice today. I really like your dress."

"Thank you, dear," Ms. Charles said. "Aren't you sweet?"

Gabrielle isn't sweet at all. She's a suck-up. I picked up my pace and rushed back to the office to see if Ms. Gloria needed any more help.

"No running in the halls!" Gabrielle yelled behind me.

"Whatever," I said as I slid into the office like I was going into home plate.

"Got anything else for me, Ms. Gloria?" I panted, trying to catch my breath.

"Nothing else today, girls."

Girls? Gabrielle was still following me like my shadow.

"Gabrielle, your mom called. She's running a little bit late, but she'll be here soon," said Ms. Gloria.

"Thank you," Gabrielle said. She sat down, crossed her legs, and waited.

I'm not sure what her mom was coming for, but I didn't want to leave her here alone, because maybe she would talk Ms. Gloria into liking her better than me. I plopped right down in the seat next to her and waited too.

"I think you would look pretty with a bow in your hair," said Gabrielle.

"Really?" I never wear anything in my hair, except a rubber band to hold it in a ponytail.

"I can tie it for you," she said.

"Okay," I agreed, trying to play it cool even though I was really, really excited.

Gabrielle got up on her knees and tied her bow around my ponytail. I shook it back and forth, and posed like I was a model in the fashion magazines that Rose reads.

"Looking good, Bean," said Ms. Gloria.

Like a burst of wind, the door swung open and in came the fanciest lady I have ever seen. She was wearing superhigh heels, a dress that looked like something a queen would wear, and so much makeup, she almost looked like a clown.

"Darling, I am so sorry I was tardy," she said as she spun around the office.

"No worries, Mother," Gabrielle said. She stood up and straightened her dress. "I have had some company while I waited."

I just sat there, slouched in my seat, with my mouth wide open. I'd never seen a lady like this before.

"Well, look at you," Gabrielle's mom stared at me with a wrinkled brow. "Aren't you a little darling for keeping my baby company?"

"Mother, this is Bean. She is in my class."

"I see," her mom said, looking me up and down like I was some sort of slob. I sat up as straight as my back would go, flattened out my T-shirt, and crossed my legs so she would stop staring at me.

"Well, then," she said, peeling her eyes off me and turning back to Gabrielle. She tugged on her dress and fluffed her hair. Then she reached into her purse, and her perfectly manicured fingers pulled out an asthma inhaler. People use that when they can't breathe very well, so maybe that's why

Gabrielle always sits on the bench during P.E. and recess. Gabrielle took it and sucked in three big, deep breaths.

"Are you feeling better?" her mom asked as she reached again into her purse. "Do you need a Motrin? A cough drop? Hand cream?"

"No, thank you, Mother."

"Sunscreen? Chapstick?"

"Mother, I am just fine."

"Well, then I'll head out. I shall see you this afternoon."

"Um, Mother? Do you think we might be able to meet outside on the playground today?" Gabrielle asked tentatively.

"No," her mother said as she shook her head in disgust. "We will meet here in the office as we always do. I cannot have you waiting out in that sun. It is very bad for the skin. Very bad for the skin, indeed. The playground is dirty . . . and all those children." She shook her head again.

"Please, Mother," pleaded Gabrielle.

"Absolutely not. See you this afternoon. A

pleasure to meet you, child," she said to me, and shook my arm, which flopped around like a noodle. Then, just as quickly as she had come in, she spun around and left.

Gabrielle's shoulders, which are usually stiff and straight, were slumped over. I felt bad for her. I mean the poor thing wasn't even allowed to play on the playground.

"Want to go see if any of the teachers need help cleaning the chalkboards?" I asked, only because I didn't have anything else to do and I did feel a little bad for Gabrielle.

We went back to our classroom, where Ms. Sullivan was sitting at her desk grading papers.

"Would you like us to clean your chalkboards and erasers, Ms. Sullivan?" I asked.

"That would be wonderful. I never get around to cleaning them."

"Goody, goody gumdrops!" Gabrielle sang.

"Leave it to us," I said.

"Thank you. I'm going to go to the teachers' lounge." Ms. Sullivan left, and we got to work.

Gabrielle wiped the boards down with a wet cloth. She was very serious about her work. I, on the other hand, was having fun slamming the erasers together and making a big cloud of dust. I danced in a circle, banging the erasers all over the place and then right in front of Gabrielle's nose.

"Stop that, Bean," Gabrielle gasped. She swatted the air and coughed.

I remembered her asthma. "Oops, sorry!" I said. I stopped right away and waved my arms so that the chalk cloud would disappear. Gabrielle kept on coughing.

I finished cleaning the erasers without making any more of a mess just as Ms. Sullivan returned.

"Thank you, girls. I think this is the cleanest my boards have ever been."

"You are very welcome," said Gabrielle, smiling, and I couldn't help but smile too.

It felt good to have Ms. Sullivan happy with me for once. And even though Gabrielle was such a goody-two-shoes, it was cool to have someone to hang out with.

"Wanna go out to the playground?" I asked hopefully.

"First stop, the bathroom," she said. "We have to wash our hands and clean up."

My hands were a little chalky. Usually, I would've just wiped them on my jeans, but if I had been wearing a dress like Gabrielle's, I wouldn't have wanted to get it dusty either.

We washed up, and since the bell hadn't rung yet, we headed out to the playground.

"Wanna climb the jungle gym?" I asked.

"No, thank you," she responded quickly, without even thinking it over.

"What about hopscotch?"

"No, Bean, I do not want to dirty my shoes," she said.

I looked at her patent leather slippers. They were pretty, but they were definitely not for running at the playground. I slumped down on the bench next to her.

"Maybe do you wanna come play at my house after school?' I asked hopefully.

"I'm not allowed to have play dates," Gabrielle told me.

She wasn't allowed to play on the playground, go to other people's houses, or even talk on the phone. What kind of a friend was that?

Maybe Bad Isn't So Bad

"Good morning, Chrysanthemum," said Gabrielle one morning when she slid next to me in line.

We'd been hanging out for a couple weeks, and she should've known my name by now. I reminded her in my most serious, I-mean-business tone of voice, "My name is Bean."

"Don't you think Chrysanthemum is a much prettier name for a girl?" she asked, all excited like she had come up with some great idea.

"No!" I yelled back. "And don't call me that!"

"Well, I just thought it might be nice if you used your pretty name and maybe wore a dress once in a while."

"No way," I said. I looked down at my jeans with the rips in the knees, my favorite Mickey Mouse sweatshirt, and my dirty sneakers. "I'm Bean and this is how I dress."

"Fine," she said. She pouted her lips and turned away.

I crossed my arms and marched to the back of the line so I wouldn't have to stand anywhere near her. I stomped past Carla and Sam without even a glance and stood behind Tanisha. The line started to move, and I dragged my feet all the way to the classroom.

"Good morning, everyone," said Ms. Sullivan. "Please take out your math books and turn to page fifteen."

I pulled out my book, but before I could open it up, I got hit in the head with a crayon. I spun around in my seat and spotted the culprit. Terrible Tanisha was chucking broken crayons! She is such a bully. I turned around and tried to focus on the first math problem.

Then another crayon hit me smack in my head. Now I was really steamed. I turned around to give her my meanest, dirtiest, nastiest glare, but—*smack!* A green crayon hit me right in my eye. Well, not really in my eye because, luckily, it was protected by my glasses.

Now, this made me so mad that I forgot how scared I was of her. I grabbed my box of pencils and erasers and stuff and scooped up all the broken bits of crayons at the bottom. I pulled my arm back like a baseball pitcher and hurled all of them at her as hard as I could.

"Chrysanthemum, what do you think you are doing?"

I froze at the sound of Ms. Sullivan's voice. I felt everyone's eyes were glued on me.

"Um . . . nothing," I said. "And it's Bean, remember?"

"Since you can't seem to remember the rules, maybe staying in for detention at recess will help refresh your memory," she said, looking sternly at me. "We do not throw crayons or anything else in this classroom."

I had never gotten a detention before, ever!

"But Tanisha was throwing crayons at me and one hit me in the head and then in my eye, well not my eye, but only because I wear glasses." Ms. Sullivan was still mad, so I kept talking. "And she wouldn't stop, so I—"

"Bean, that's enough."

"But, Ms. Sullivan . . . ," I groaned as I dropped my head onto my cold desk. Then she called on Stanley, who was raising his hand.

"It's true," he said timidly. "Tanisha started it. She was throwing crayons. One hit me too."

"I wasn't throwin' nothing," Tanisha growled.

I turned around in my seat and gave Stanley a big thank-you smile. It was supercool of him to have my back, even though Tanisha would definitely clobber him after school.

"Thank you, Stanley," Ms. Sullivan said. "Looks like Bean and Tanisha will both be in detention during recess."

"But," I said, "that's not fair. She started it."

Ms. Sullivan ignored me and said, "Everyone

please get back to work."

The room settled down, but I couldn't do my math problems, because Tanisha was glaring at me from across the room with fire in her eyes.

The rest of the morning was awful. All I could think about was detention, as I watched the hands of the clock move. Finally, the bell rang and everyone jumped out of their seats, like they always do before Ms. Sullivan could even say, "Recess!"

"Okay, ladies," Ms. Sullivan said to me and Tanisha. "Stay in your seats while I take the rest of the class to the playground."

I stood up, though, and walked toward her. "I can't stay in for recess because . . . um . . ." I stopped for a second and tried to think of a good excuse. Then I remembered Gabrielle's asthma. "The doctor said I need fresh air or . . . um . . . my lungs will explode and then I'll puff up like a balloon and maybe even die."

"Bean, when you break the rules, you must pay the consequences," Ms. Sullivan said to me, like she didn't even care about my lung problem. "Sit down, because you are staying in for recess."

And just like that, she left the room and so did all the kids and I was left all alone with Terrible Tanisha. I hoped Ms. Sullivan would come back soon. I'm not a scaredy-cat, but Tanisha is c-r-a-z-y CRAZY!

"I'm gonna make you wish my name never came out your mouth," Tanisha said. She circled my chair and poked me with her pencil.

"You started it."

"I'm gonna make your life miserable," she said. She shoved me to the floor. But just as her fist flew at my head, the classroom door swung open.

"What is going on in here?" bellowed Ms. Sullivan.

I kept my mouth shut, because I knew that if I tattled again, Tanisha was gonna kill me for sure.

"Bean, answer me," she said, like she knew Tanisha had knocked me down.

"I fell," I said.

"Are you sure?"

"Yes, ma'am."

"All right, then," said Ms. Sullivan said as she sat at her desk. "Get back in your seats. I want you to write *I will not throw crayons* twenty-five times."

I didn't want to get in any more trouble, so I moved quickly. I pulled out a paper and started writing in my squiggly, not-so-great handwriting. *I will not throw crayons. I will not throw crayons.* Tanisha started writing too, but every time Ms. Sullivan looked away, Tanisha stared at me with an I'm-going-to-kill-you kinda look.

"I have to use the bathroom, but I'm going to leave the door open and I don't want any more trouble. Do you understand?"

"Yes, Ms. Sullivan," I said, wishing she wouldn't leave us alone again.

Just as she stepped out of sight, another crayon came flying through the air and hit me in the back of my head.

I will not throw crayons. I will not throw crayons. I kept writing.

Tanisha got up from her seat and started moving around the room. I tried to focus on writing, but I couldn't help but sneak a peek. I spotted Tanisha squirting paste onto Stanley's chair. When I looked again, she was chomping on a huge piece of bubblegum. She blew a huge bubble and then stuck it right in Gabrielle's spelling book. Next, she hopped over to Aisha's desk and drew hearts that said, "I Love Stanley!" on it with a red marker.

Now, I know it's not a good idea to write on tables and put gum in books and paste on chairs, but you have to admit it was kind of funny and really brave of her. I would never have the nerve to do stuff like that.

Tanisha saw me smile, and I guess it made her not want to kill me so bad, because she left me alone. She rushed to her seat right as Ms. Sullivan came inside, and we both got back to writing.

It took forever to finish twenty-five lines of *I will not throw crayons,* but I got the last one done just as the bell rang and everyone came into the room.

I spent the rest of the day waiting for someone to mention Tanisha's pranks, but no one did. Stanley went home sick after lunch, so the paste on his chair dried up. We had already had spelling in the morning, so Gabrielle didn't notice that the pages of her book were all stuck together. I saw Aisha scrubbing her desk with a tissue, but she must have been too embarrassed to say anything.

A crayon flew through the air and hit Sam right in the back of the head. *Ha!* Served her right for stealing my best friend. I looked over at Tanisha and she was smiling. Our eyes met and she winked at me. I smiled and winked back. Maybe Tanisha wasn't so bad after all.

8

The Dinosaurs Are Closed

TGIF! That means "Thank God it's Friday," and boy, do I love Fridays! Mostly, I think they are great because it's almost the weekend, but today was even better because my class was going on a field trip to the Natural History Museum!

When Ms. Sullivan first told us about the trip, I was a little worried. I mean, who was I gonna sit with on the bus? Not Carla. Not Stinky Stanley and definitely not Terrible Tanisha. But then I had a great idea. Since Mom has Fridays off from work, I asked her to be a chaperone and—guess what? She said yes! My mom is the best.

As soon as I woke up, I got dressed and headed to the bathroom. I bumped right into Mom.

"Good morning," she said with a weird look on her face.

"How come you're wearing your hospital scrubs?" I asked.

"Baby, I have some bad news." She knelt down in front of me and looked right into my eyes. "I got a call from the hospital and they need me to come to work."

"But you don't work on Fridays. It's your day off."

"I know, but Nurse Johnson and Nurse Manning are both sick."

"Can't you tell them that you're sick too?" I pleaded.

"No, baby, I can't. That wouldn't be true, and besides, they need me," she said. "I already called the school to let them know."

"But you promised."

"I know and I'm sorry." Mom gave me a hug. "I'll

make it up to you this weekend. Maybe we can go for ice cream, just you and me."

"I hate ice cream," I said as I stomped off to the bathroom. I brushed my teeth, washed my face, and dragged my feet downstairs to the kitchen. Dad was at the table eating scrambled eggs.

"Can you chaperone the school trip today, Dad?" I asked, squeezing him so tight around his shoulders that he couldn't lift his fork to his mouth.

"Sorry, baby. I have classes all day at the college."

I slumped down in a seat at the table between Rose and Gardenia and scooped a spoonful of eggs into my mouth.

"Come on, Bean. We're gonna be late," Rose said.

"Bye, girls! Have a good day," Dad called as Rose dragged me and Gardenia out the door.

"Doubt it," I groaned to myself.

I was not so excited for the trip anymore and not so thankful that it was Friday. ISMIF! That stands for "I'm So Mad it's Friday!"

"See ya later," Rose said as she dropped me off at

the number 3 spot on the playground.

I waved good-bye to her and got on the line. Right as I passed Terrible Tanisha, she stuck her foot out to try and trip me. Luckily, I spotted it just in time and hopped over it. Tanisha stuck her foot out again when Gabrielle skipped past. She's not as quick as me, so she tripped. She stumbled and scuffed her shiny shoes on the pavement. I couldn't help but giggle when she pulled a little cloth from her purse and began polishing them.

Ms. Sullivan called roll and then we walked over to a big yellow bus. I had a pit in my stomach. Who was I gonna sit next to?

Gabrielle was the first to get on the bus, then John, then Sam. When it was finally my turn, I climbed up the big, huge steps. Luckily, I spotted an empty row right behind Ms. Sullivan. Sitting alone wouldn't be too bad. At least I wouldn't have to beg someone to let me sit next to them.

Tanisha was the last to get on. She looked around and there were no more empty rows. She was gonna have to sit next to someone.

"Please find a seat, Tanisha," called Ms. Sullivan. "Time to go."

I crossed my fingers and hoped that she wouldn't sit in my row. But sure enough, she plopped herself down next to me and stared right at me. Take a picture, it will last longer, I thought to myself, but I didn't dare say it out loud. Instead, I leaned my head against the cool window and watched the cars and trucks and motorcycles zoom by.

We pulled up to the Natural History Museum, and, boy, did that change my mood. I had never seen dinosaurs in real life, and Ms. Sullivan said that they have a room full of them. I was excited!

Everyone piled out of the bus in front of the big white building, and we all lined up by the stairs. A lady met us. She said, "I'm Ms. John," which was funny because John is a man's name. She was also wearing a red bow tie, which was really funny because ties are definitely for men, not women. She talked in a low whispery voice that didn't go up and down like normal people's do and she never stopped talking the whole time, not even when she was walking.

And she refused to answer my questions, even when I raised my hand and waved it around right in front of her.

We looked at junk in glass boxes that Ms. John called artifacts. B-o-r-i-n-g BORING! But, then I saw something shocking. Right there in broad daylight was a clay sculpture of a naked lady, about the size of a Barbie doll, on a table. Tanisha came up beside me.

"That's your favorite thing in the whole museum!" she teased.

"No. I'm just looking at it because it's old and it's art, you know."

"Don't look at her boooooooobies!" While no one was looking, Terrible Tanisha dropped a tissue on the naked statue's head.

I tried my hardest to stop myself from giggling, but I couldn't. The statue was almost all covered, except for the feet, and she looked like someone dressed as a ghost on Halloween.

When I turned, Tanisha was nowhere to be found. I didn't want anyone to think I had done it, so I hightailed it out of there.

At lunch, we sat around a long table in the cafeteria. I sat at the very end, right next to Sam, who sat next to Carla, who still was acting as if I didn't exist.

"This trip is pretty great, huh?" I said to Sam, but she didn't hear because she was too busy listening to Carla.

Ms. Sullivan and Ms. John passed out brown-paper-bag lunches with carrots—*yuck*—cheese sandwiches—*yum*—and cookies—*double yum!* Just as I finished my sandwich, I noticed Tanisha wasn't across from me anymore. I peeked under the table, and there she was, with a big smile on her face. We both popped up just as Ms. Sullivan called, "Finish eating and throw out your trash."

Everyone got up to go . . . except Sam. She tripped and tumbled to the floor. Her shoelaces were tied together! Everyone laughed as she struggled to untie them and collect her lunch from the floor. I laughed harder than anyone else, because I knew who had done it. I turned and looked right at Tanisha and she grinned at me. I know she's mean, but she is kinda funny.

"Ms. Sullivan, can I go to the bathroom?" I asked.

"Sure, Bean. Take a partner and meet us by the stairs."

I looked around. I had no one to be partners with and this was an emergency! I really needed to pee.

"Renee, will you go to the bathroom with me?" I asked.

"I don't have to go," she said, and then just walked away.

"Sam, will you go with me to the bathroom?"

"Naw, I just went," she said.

I don't think she understood how serious this was. I really had to go to the bathroom. I crossed my legs and wiggled around as I looked for someone else.

"I'll go with you," said Tanisha, and she started marching toward the bathroom. I had no other choice at this point, so I followed her. I burst through the door of the bathroom and into the first stall. *Ahh!*

Tanisha was at the sink pumping pink, foamy

soap into her hand. She kept pumping and pumping till it looked like a pile of cotton candy.

"Cool," I said, and squirted a pile of pink into my hand too. I rubbed my hands together and stuck them under the water to wash them, but not Terrible Tanisha. She slapped her hand onto the mirror, covering it with pink bubbles.

"Your turn," she said as she started pumping another pile of soap into her hand.

"No, thanks. My hands are already clean."

I pushed the button on the hand dryer, and hot air blew like a tornado and dried my hands. When I turned around, both mirrors were covered in soap bubbles and Tanisha was standing in a stall shoving toilet paper into the toilet.

"Come on," she called. "Help me out."

I went closer and watched as she threw piles and piles of paper into the water. I grabbed a handful of those paper toilet-seat covers and dropped them in too. She gave me a high five and—*flush!* The paper churned and gurgled in the toilet, and then water started exploding everywhere.

Tanisha howled with laughter, but I spun around and ran as fast as I could out of the bathroom, down the main hall, and to the stairs. I didn't stop till I almost crashed into Ms. Sullivan and the rest of the class.

"No running in the museum," scolded Ms. John.

"Yes, ma'am," I said. My heart was still pounding, but I tried to stay calm as we walked through the butterfly exhibit.

"Attention, please, museum patrons," a loudspeaker announced. "Due to a flood in the main hall, the dinosaur and fossil halls will be closed for the remainder of the day."

No way! Now I would never get to see the T. rex, the triceratops, or the flying one that I don't remember the name of. This was all my fault. I dragged my feet through the rest of the museum, not even looking at anything. Well, maybe I peeked a little in the mammals' hall, which was filled with funny-looking cavemen who looked like they were about kill a stuffed bear.

At the end of the day, we got on the bus and

headed back to school. Tanisha sat next to me again, but I just ignored her. I leaned against the window, closed my eyes, and just felt sad. Clogging the toilet was a really b-a-d BAD idea.

9

He'll Never Catch Us

After school, my sisters were busy giggling with their friends and flirting with boys, so I had to wait to go home. I leaned against the fence with my arms crossed and watched the crowds of kids scatter. It wouldn't have been so bad if Carla and Sam weren't shooting hoops and looking like they were having a ton of fun.

Tanisha crossed the playground, dragging her dirty backpack on the cement. Instead of heading to the open gate, she walked straight toward me.

"Whatcha doin'?" she asked, like we were friends.

"Waiting for my sisters." I motioned toward them.

"Well, wanna hang out?" she asked matter-of-factly. "I'm bored."

I just stared at her, confused.

"I'll show you the drawer where Ms. Sullivan keeps all the candy she takes away from us," Tanisha added.

Now this was something I wanted to see. I mean, I l-o-v-e LOVE candy, and plus, maybe Carla would see us and get jealous.

We walked back toward the building, past Carla and Sam, who didn't even seem to notice. Rose didn't either. Her eyes were glued to Doug, a tall, good-looking boy who was picking up his little sister from kindergarten. Me and Tanisha slid right past them and walked into the building.

The door shut behind us. We were all alone in the school. It was quiet and kinda weird to be in the dark, empty halls. Tanisha pulled out two huge gumballs and handed me one. I chomped on it like a horse, with my mouth wide open. Mmm . . . cherry flavor!

"Watch this," Tanisha said. She pulled out the big red wad and stuck it over the hole of the water fountain. When she turned the knob, water sprayed from the spout like a sprinkler all over the hall. I jumped out of the way just in time!

As we kept walking, Tanisha dragged a purple marker along the wall, making a squiggly line. Now, this made me really nervous. Students are not supposed to be in the building after school, and for sure we aren't supposed to draw on the walls. Tanisha stopped at another water fountain right in front of our classroom.

"Your turn." She nudged me in the side.

"Naw. It's okay."

"Girl, do it!" Tanisha demanded; then she pushed me toward the fountain.

I thought about it for a second. If I did it and got caught, I would be in big trouble, but if I didn't, Tanisha might reach into my mouth and get it herself. So I went for it . . . I spit the wad of gum onto my fingers, shoved it over the hole of the fountain, took a deep breath, and turned the knob. No water came out.

"You blocked the whole thing." Tanisha laughed. "Move it to the side."

I dug my finger in and wiggled it around a little. When I turned the knob, water sprayed everywhere, and this time, we didn't make it out of the way—water sprinkled all over us.

"Hey! What are you two doing in here?" Mr. Hopper, the janitor, yelled from down the hall.

"We're okay," said Tanisha as she grabbed my hand. "He's so fat, he'll never catch us."

"Get back here!" Mr. Hopper yelled as he ran behind us, huffing and puffing and dragging a bucket and mop.

We turned the corner and pushed through the door and into Ms. Ring's classroom. I could barely breathe. It was totally empty and quiet, and I remembered how safe I used to feel when I was in Ms. Ring's class. I never ever got into trouble. I was a good girl then, but now I wasn't so sure.

Tanisha peered out the door.

No Mr. Hopper, so she dragged me back into the hall. Just as we reached the big red door to go outside, Mr. Hopper popped his big head around the corner and yelled, "Get back here, you troublemakers!"

I flew through the door and ran right to Rose's side.

"Bean, where have you been?" she asked.

"We had to use the bathroom."

"Next time, let me know."

"All right," I said, but I had absolutely no plans of running through the halls after school ever again.

"Let's go," said Rose. She turned and headed toward the gate, where Gardenia was waiting.

"Hey, Bean, can you come over and play for a little while?" Tanisha asked.

"Maybe," I said, to give me time to think. I hadn't had a play date since school started and I guessed it would be kinda fun to play with someone . . . even if it was Tanisha. "Let me ask my sister." I ran to catch Rose. "Do you think it would be okay if I go over to Tanisha's house for a little bit?"

Tanisha ran up too and said, "I live just down the block from you, by Jackson's Barbershop."

"Let me talk to you for a second," Rose said to me as she pulled me away from Tanisha. "Since when are you two pals?"

"Since now."

"Bean, you know Tanisha is bad news and you always said she was mean to you." Rose looked doubtful. "I don't think it's a good idea."

"Please," I begged. "I finally have someone to play with and she's really not so bad."

"Fine," she said with a shrug. "But you better be home before dark."

I agreed, and we all started walking toward home. Tanisha was smiling. I don't think she ever had anyone over for a play date. She told me she has no sisters, and I definitely knew she didn't have any friends.

Tanisha's apartment building was tucked in the alley. It was right behind Jackson's Barbershop, with the swirly red-and-white pole that looks like a candy cane. I'd been to Jackson's once with Dad to get his hair cut. I never knew Tanisha lived so close by. My house was down the block, but this part of the neighborhood felt completely different.

"Remember, no street crossing without an adult, and be home before dark!" Rose yelled over her shoulder as she disappeared around the corner.

I followed Tanisha to her building and up the stairs. The halls were dark and dirty and it kinda smelled like garbage and dog pee and smoke. The floorboards squeaked under my sneakers as we turned down a dark hallway and finally got to her door.

Tanisha reached in her shirt and pulled out a key on a black string that was hanging around her neck and unlocked the door. I wondered where her mom was. I didn't think she had a father. Well, I guess she's gotta have one because that's how babies are made, but she's never talked about him at school. It made me feel so happy I have a dad. Come to think of it, I was glad to have sisters too, because Tanisha must get lonely.

I trailed behind Tanisha as we walked inside. It was cold, but Tanisha didn't seem to notice.

"Want a snack or something?" she asked.

"Sure. Whatcha got?"

I stood in the middle of the room. It seemed like the whole house was in that one room. It was the kitchen and also the living room and maybe even the bedroom too. The stove, refrigerator, and sink were on one side, next to a table and a pullout couch made up like a bed, with a small TV on the other side.

"How about some Cheetos?"

"Sure!"

I loosened up a little bit because Cheetos are my favorite, you know. She opened the bag and sat down on the couch bed. I sat on the edge and dug my hand in the bag. I popped a couple Cheetos in my mouth. Yum!

Tanisha turned on a small staticky TV and we watched cartoons through the fuzz.

"Want me to show you something cool?" Tanisha asked.

"Okay," I said as she dragged me into a room with another unmade bed in the middle and nothing much else.

Tanisha got down on her hands and knees and pulled a box from under the bed. I sat next to her on the floor so I could get a look at what was inside—shiny necklaces, a pack of stinky cigarettes, and a whole bunch of money in a pile. More money than I had ever seen in one place.

"Your mom should put that in the bank."

"She goes to the bank every Monday," Tanisha said, and put two dollar bills in her back pocket. "I'm not supposed to know it's here."

"What time does your mom get home?" I asked, because it was getting kind of creepy being here. I had never been in a house with no adults. Someone is always home at my house.

"Usually, my mom gets home after dark, but it depends," said Tanisha softly. She got up off the floor and looked out the window.

"I think I better go," I said. "I promised my dad I would help with dinner."

"You've gotta stay here for dinner," she barked, but I insisted I had to go. I rushed to the front door as fast as I could.

"I really can't!" I called over my shoulder. I didn't stop walking, because I was a little worried that she would grab me, tie me up, and force me to stay.

I ran all the way home and felt much better when I swung through the back door and saw my dad. I wrapped my arms around his middle and gave him a good, long squeeze.

10 Caught

Wednesday began just like every other morning. I got dressed, washed up, and headed downstairs to the kitchen for breakfast. The whole family was at the table like usual, but then we heard a knock.

Gardenia raced up and swung open the door. No way! Stinky Stanley was standing there with a big, silly smile on his face.

"Bean, your boyfriend is here," Gardenia said.

"He's not my boyfriend!"

"Hi, Bean," Stanley said as he stepped into the

kitchen. "Hi, Mr. Gibson."

"What are you doing here?" I asked.

"I just stopped by to pick up my saxophone. Your dad was gonna fix it for me."

"All fixed," Dad said as he pointed to the leather case, which was propped up against the door. "Why don't you try it and see how the keys feel?"

"All right," said Stanley. He dropped his backpack, grabbed the case, and followed Dad into the living room.

"Bean, go grab your violin and come too," Dad suggested.

"Now? With him?"

"Yes," he said sternly. "Now."

I know better than to argue with Dad when he talks serious like that, so I went up to my room and pulled my violin case out from under the bed. I sat at the top of the stairs, listening to Stanley putting his saxophone together and blowing to test the keys.

"Bean?" Dad yelled.

"Coming," I moaned.

I walked as slow as I could. I put my case on the couch, all the way on the other side of the room from Stanley. I didn't want to sit too close, you know. A person could die from his stink.

"Okay guys, you have a couple minutes to play till breakfast is ready." And with that, Dad went back into the kitchen and left me alone with Stanley.

"That's pretty cool that you play the violin," he said.

"Well, I'm just learning."

"I am too."

"No, I mean I'm really just learning. The first day I played, it sounded like I was killin' a cat."

Stanley blew into his saxophone and—*blaaaag!* The most awful noise exploded. I laughed so hard I nearly dropped my violin on the floor. I knew he did it on purpose to make me feel better—and it really did!

Then Stanley played real notes and I followed the best I could by pressing the strings and pulling the bow and—guess what? Playing with Stanley was kind of fun. Reading sheet music was still hard for me, but I was getting pretty good at playing along with notes that I could hear.

"Why don't you guys come in and eat some breakfast," Dad said as he stuck his head through the door.

We put away our instruments and headed into the kitchen. Stanley grabbed his backpack. It was bright red with a cool race car on it.

"Is that new?" I asked.

"Yep, I just got it yesterday."

"That car is supercool," I let him know.

"Thanks."

I sat next to Stanley at breakfast, and he wasn't so stinky after all. Maybe he just seemed smellier before because that's what everyone at school always said. Maybe the rumors had crept into my nose. I mean, he kinda had a smelly-feet-need-a-shower kinda stink, but nothing that was gonna make you fall out of the chair and die, you know.

Stanley walked to school with me, Rose, and Gardenia. Me and Stanley laughed as we tried to kick a rock like a soccer ball. We had to keep it from falling off the sidewalk and into the street.

When we got to school, I wasn't so sure that I wanted everyone to think me and Stanley were friends. I gave him one last smile and then, with a shrug of my shoulders, I ran ahead and slid in line next to Tanisha.

"Happy hump day!" I said to her.

"What's that mean?"

"My dad calls Wednesday hump day because it's in the middle of the week, which means that when it's finished, you're over the hump and on the home stretch to the weekend. And boy, am I glad it's hump day!"

Tanisha just shrugged. She doesn't get excited about stuff like that.

The line started to move, and I skipped all the way into the building. Goody-two-shoes Gabrielle was the door holder. Me and Tanisha made faces at her as we passed.

"You two are unkempt goons," Gabrielle said.

I don't know what *unkempt* means, but I know what *goon* does and it is not very nice at all. When Gabrielle passed by us to take her place back in line,

Tanisha stuck out her foot and—*trip!* Gabrielle tumbled to the floor.

"Oww!" she moaned as she got up and wiped off her frilly pink dress.

Tanisha howled with laughter. Gabrielle hadn't hurt herself, so I giggled too and gave Tanisha a high five.

During morning lessons, Ms. Sullivan let me and Tanisha share a social studies book. While I was trying to read, she kept folding the pages. Then she blew a spitball right at me. In spelling, she even cheated off my test. I liked having someone to hang out with, but Tanisha was driving me crazy! Carla was a real friend. She would never do anything mean. At least that's how it used to be.

The bell rang for recess, and as I got up from my seat, I bumped right into Carla.

"Wanna play hopscotch?" I asked hopefully.

"No, thank you, Bean." Carla turned her back to me and headed into the hallway, pulling Sam along with her.

"I brought Flamin' Hot Cheetos," I yelled,

swinging the bag in the air. "You want some?"

"I've got my own bag," Carla said. She didn't smile, but at least she had talked to me.

Tanisha grabbed my arm and dragged me to the playground.

"Let's throw rocks at cars," she said.

"No way. We'll get in big trouble." I was not planning on going to jail that day or any other day!

"Scaredy-cat!"

"Am not," I said, "but I'm also not stupid."

"Yeah, you are!" She shoved me and ran off across the playground. I felt kinda mad that she still bullied me, but not mad enough to stop playing, so I ran after her.

"Let's mess with those girls." She pointed at Renee and Aisha, who were playing hopscotch. We danced on the hopscotch board so they had to stop playing.

Finally Aisha whined, "Leave us alone!"

We grabbed a basketball from some boys and threw it over the fence. I laughed along with Tanisha, but way down deep, I didn't feel right. I tried to ignore the twisting in my tummy, though, because for the first time in a long time, I had someone to play with.

"Come on, Bean," said Tanisha as she stomped her feet in a big, dirty puddle, right next to where Gabrielle was sitting on the bench reading.

I just stood there, because I didn't want to mess with anyone else today and I for sure didn't want to get my socks and sneakers all soaking wet. But Tanisha gave me a growly I-mean-business look and dragged me into the puddle.

"Now my feet are all wet, Tanisha!"

She just laughed as she splashed around in the water. Tanisha pointed at Gabrielle and gave me a wink. Before I could stop her, she swung her leg, and dirty, muddy water sprinkled on Gabrielle's dress and mud speckled her white ruffled socks.

Gabrielle got up and ran into the building. I sloshed out of the puddle, feeling terrible. The bell rang and everyone started filing off the playground. Tanisha grabbed my arm again and pulled me so fast that my soaking wet feet barely touched the ground.

"Where are we going?" I said, running to try and keep up. If I didn't, she probably would've dragged me right across the cement.

"I have a plan, but we've gotta hurry." Tanisha dragged me through the red door.

"This is the big plan? To get into the building first?"

"No, silly! We're gonna hide behind the door and . . ." Just as Tanisha was explaining her plan, someone pushed the door and *slam!* Tanisha shoved it back as hard as she could. I could hear the sound of the door hitting someone.

"Ha! We got 'em good!" She laughed. But I didn't because I could hear crying from the other side of the door.

I slowly opened the door to see the damage. A girl was lying on the floor covering her face. She looked up at me with blood dripping from her nose and tears in her eyes. Oh, no! It was Carla.

"You're bleeding!" I cried in shock.

Sam pointed at me and yelled, "Bean, what did you do?"

Ms. Sullivan came running to see what all the commotion was.

"What's your problem? That was really mean!" Sam barked at me with fire in her eyes.

"It wasn't me!" I swore.

"What happened?" Ms. Sullivan asked.

Before I could say a word, Sam told Ms. Sullivan, "Bean slammed the door as we were coming in and it hit Carla in the face and she did it on purpose!"

"Bean, go straight to the principal's office," said Ms. Sullivan angrily as she led Carla to the nurse's office with Sam following. "This is unacceptable behavior and I will not stand for it."

When I was all alone, Tanisha popped her stupid head around the corner.

"Are they gone?" she said.

"You have to tell them you did it!" I cried.

"I'm not the one who got caught. You were," Tanisha said. She leaned against the wall like it was no big deal.

I was so fuming mad that I wanted to scream.

11

Grounded

"Sit down by Mr. Bloodsoe's door," Ms. Gloria said without a smile.

This wasn't the Ms. Gloria I knew, but I guess I seemed like a very different Bean to her too.

I flopped into the chair and waited for Mr. Bloodsoe. I couldn't stop shaking. Mr. Bloodsoe is scary. He's so hairy that even his neck is covered. His eyes bulge out of his skull and his teeth are pointy like daggers. He looks like an ogre who lives in a cave.

Creeeak! The door to his office slowly opened. I covered my mouth so I wouldn't scream as he lumbered toward me.

"This way," growled Mr. Bloodsoe. He motioned with his big, thick, hairy arm. He walked into the office behind me and sat at his huge, messy desk.

"It wasn't . . . um . . . I didn't . . . This is all a big mistake. I promise to be good and . . . um . . . I won't be bad anymore," I stammered. Then I smiled my warmest please-forgive-me smile.

"If you didn't do it, then who did?" he growled.

I zipped my lips because I knew I couldn't tattle. Tanisha would kill me for sure.

"This is not like you, Chrysanthemum. We've never had any problems with you before."

"And you won't ever have any again. I promise I'll be good and I'll listen and I'll . . ." I kept babbling on, but I stopped short when Mr. Bloodsoe picked up the phone. Was he gonna call security to haul me away? The cops to arrest me?

"I'm going to have to call your parents," he said.

Oh no! That was even worse. Tears started to

creep into my eyes as he pressed one number at a time. I hoped and hoped and hoped that no one would answer, but no luck.

"Hello, Mr. Gibson, sir. This is Mr. Bloodsoe from Coliseum Elementary. I have Chrysanthemum here in my office. She has been giving her teacher some problems."

I buried my face in my hands.

"Yes, Ms. Sullivan said that she's been throwing things and talking back in class, and today, a little girl was hurt badly because of her mischief."

He had it all wrong! None of this was my fault.

"Thank you, sir. I am sure you will," Mr. Bloodsoe said as he hung up the phone and turned to me. "If Ms. Sullivan has any more problems with you, there are going to be some serious consequences, Chrysanthemum. Do you understand?"

I didn't think this was a good time to tell him that my name is actually Bean. Instead, I nodded and said, "Yes, sir. I will be a good girl. I promise."

The minute he stood up, I rushed out of the office. I was too embarrassed to look at Ms. Gloria. I headed right back to class. Ms. Sullivan gave me an angry glare as I slid into my seat.

I felt really, really superbad when I saw that Carla's seat was empty. I looked over at Terrible Tanisha and she was smiling to herself. She was definitely not going to be my friend anymore. I would rather be alone forever.

I made it through the rest of the day without even opening my mouth. When the bell finally rang, I lined up and tried to be invisible as the class walked to the playground.

"Bean, may I speak to you for a second?" Ms. Sullivan asked before I could make it over to Rose, who was waiting by the fence.

"Yes, ma'am," I said, trying to be as polite as I could.

"I would like you to think about your behavior and how it affects others. Carla got hurt today."

"Yes, ma'am."

"And you will have to stay in for recess for the rest of the week," she added.

"Yes, ma'am," I agreed, even though it made me

really sad. I said good-bye and headed over to Rose.

"What was all that about, Bean?" she asked. "Ms. Sullivan looked upset."

"Tanisha slammed Carla with the door and she got really hurt. They blamed me and I got in big trouble."

Tears started rolling down my cheeks again. I tried to hold them in my eyes, but it was no use. Rose put her arm around my shoulder. I must have really looked upset, because even Gardenia didn't make fun of me as we walked home.

I slowed to a snail's crawl as I spotted the house up ahead. I didn't wanna face Dad. When we got there, Rose swung the door open and I crept in, snuck to the computer, and plopped myself down. I needed to email Tanya, but before I could even log on, Dad came down the stairs.

"No computer!" he barked.

I couldn't even get a word out before he was shuffling me up the stairs and into my room.

"No TV and no playing outside. We will talk about this when your mother gets home," Dad said.

He shut the door, and he didn't leave it open a crack like he usually does.

I dropped my backpack and sprawled across my bed. I couldn't stop thinking about poor Carla. I hoped her nose wasn't broken. What if she had to go to the hospital? What if my mom saw her there?

My head was spinning, but I finally finished my homework. Then I braided my doll's hair, stared at the wall, and flipped through my Ramona book. I could hear Rose and her friend Gina playing hop-scotch outside. I wished I could go out and play with them, even though they wouldn't have let me anyway.

I could hear Gardenia practicing her flute downstairs. That's it! Maybe I could practice my violin to keep my mind off things. Dad had taught me the scales, and I could almost get through them without screeching. I took my violin out and started playing the notes over and over and over again.

"Dad told me to deliver this to you," Rose said as she placed a tray on the table next to my bed. Chicken noodle soup and grilled cheese—*yum!* But not so yummy when you have to eat it all alone in your bedroom.

"This is my fault," she said before she left. "I knew I shouldn't have let you hang out with that girl."

"No, it's not. It's my fault. I was just so lonely without Carla, you know."

"I know," she said, then headed back downstairs.

I plopped myself down on the floor and ate my grilled cheese. Dad had made it just right. I dipped the grilled cheese in the soup and gobbled it all up. When I was done, I got back to practicing the violin. I played and played and played . . . anything to stop thinking about Carla.

It was getting late. It must have been almost bedtime, which meant that Mom was sure to be home any minute. I started getting nervous. What if Mom and Dad didn't believe me? What if they yelled and screamed? What if they got so mad, they made me go live at Grand Mommy's?

I went to the bathroom and washed my face,

brushed my teeth, and put on my favorite pajamas with the clouds on them. And waited. Just as I climbed into bed, Mom and Dad came into my room. Dad still looked mad and Mom looked worried. I don't know which made me feel worse.

"Bean, we are very disappointed," Dad started. "You have always been such a good girl."

"What's going on, baby?" said Mom. She sat on the edge of my bed.

"It was all a big mistake. I missed Tanya and Carla, and I thought being friends with Tanisha was a good idea, but it wasn't."

The tears started to fall from my eyes and down onto my sheets. I told Mom and Dad everything while Mom wrapped her arms around me and held me tight.

"I'm so sorry," I cried. "I messed up big-time."

"It's okay to make mistakes as long as we learn and grow from them," Dad said.

I didn't think I had grown any bigger, but I had learned for sure.

"I'll be better. I promise."

"And tomorrow you have to tell Carla how sorry you are," Mom said as she gave me a warm hug.

"I will," I agreed.

"You're still grounded for the rest of the week," Dad said. "No computer. No TV. No playing outside."

I didn't want to be grounded, but before they left, Dad hugged me too, so I knew everything was gonna be all right.

They turned out the lights and closed the door. This time, they left it open just a crack like I like it.

I tossed and turned all night. I was scared to face Carla. The night seemed to last forever, but still the sun came up too soon. I covered my head with my blanket to block my eyes from the sun rays. I was hoping I could hide there for the rest of third grade.

"Bean, get up!" Gardenia yelled.

"*Ughh . . . ,*" I moaned, hoping she would leave me alone.

"What's wrong with you?" She yanked the covers off my head.

"I'm sick!" I said, thinking fast.

"No, you're not. Now get out of bed, so you don't make us all late."

"*Aggggh . . . uggggh . . .*" I winced, using my best acting skills. I was the star of the second-grade holiday play last year, you know. Okay, maybe not the actual star, but I played the star at the top of the tree, which was a very important role.

"I think Bean isn't feeling well," Gardenia called out to Dad.

"What's wrong?" he asked as he placed his warm hand on my head.

"My head is killing me. My stomach feels icky. My eyes are blurry and my hangnails are hurting!"

"Wow!" Dad exclaimed, surprised at how sick I was. "We'd better get your mother to come check on you."

Mom's a nurse, as you know, so she was gonna be much harder to fool than Dad.

"You're not feeling well, baby?" Mom slid into bed next to me.

I squinted my eyes and hugged my knees as I listed my symptoms again. This time, I threw in a cough and a couple moans and groans for effect.

"Looks to me like you've got a severe case of Gooblety Gash."

"Sounds serious," said Dad.

"Is she gonna die?" Gardenia asked.

Maybe I really was sick with Gooblety Gash. I was too young to die! My head started to pound. My hands shook and my stomach twisted and turned. I was sick!

"We need to take you right to the hospital and get you into surgery or this could be fatal," Mom said.

"I don't want to have surgery!" I yelled. I hopped out of bed and jumped up and down.

"All you've got is a severe case of I Don't Want to Go to School," Mom said, laughing. "You've got to be strong and face your fears."

"Whoa . . . wait a second," I said, but then I got it. "Fine." I pouted as I stomped to the bathroom to get ready for school.

12

It's Hard to Say I'm Sorry

When we got to school, that sick feeling came back, right in my stomach.

"I have to stay after school today to work on a science project. Wait on the playground till I get there to pick you up. Okay?" Rose said.

I was scared to face Carla. I shook my head no and held Rose tight.

"You're gonna be fine," she said when she finally pried herself loose. "See you later."

I watched Rose disappear, then walked straight

to Ms. Sullivan to apologize, but nothing seemed to come from my lips.

"What is it, Bean?" she asked.

"I, um . . . well, see, sorry . . . 'cause, you know." The words got all jumbled and nothing made sense. She just stared down at me like I was crazy, patted me on the shoulder, and told me to go line up. I decided to try again tomorrow when the thoughts in my head weren't so scrambled.

I spotted Carla. Her nose was all red and swollen and there was a big pink Band-Aid on her face. I tried to think of the right words to say as I got closer, but I couldn't seem to find them. I looked at my toes as I walked past her.

All day, I tried to stay as far from Carla and Sam as I could. I wanted to say I was sorry, but I didn't know how.

Tanisha was being extra mean to me too. She tripped me in the hall, broke my pencil, and knocked all my books on the floor. I knew she just wanted to be friends again, but she sure had a funny way of showing it.

At lunch, I had no one to sit with. Gardenia was at a crowded table full of giggling fifth graders. I walked up with my lunch bag, but she just turned her back to me and kept laughing with her friends. Gardenia is probably the worst sister on planet Earth.

I scanned the room for another seat. I spotted an empty table right by the door, but just as I was about to plop myself down, Gabrielle shimmied onto the bench. I stopped. I hadn't said one word to her since the muddy-water incident, and I still felt really awful.

"Hello, Bean," she said, like she wasn't even mad at me.

"Hello," I said tentatively, in case this was a trick or something.

"Would you like to sit with me for lunch?"

"Okay," I said, but I was confused. Why was she being so nice?

"I'm not mad at you anymore," Gabrielle said. "My mother said that *forgiveness is next to godliness,* so I let it go. But you better not do anything like that again or I may not be so *godly.*"

"I promise," I said sincerely. "I really am sorry."

I slid into the seat across from her and pulled out my ham sandwich, red Jell-O, and juice box. Gabrielle pulled out a plastic bowl of icky green salad with stinky pink fish on the top.

"Ugh!" I scrunched up my nose. "I don't eat anything green and definitely nothing smelly from the ocean."

"Green things are good for you and so is fish," she said, but then I saw her glance at my food hungrily. "My mom won't let me eat anything unhealthy."

I watched her stab her fork into her lettuce as I chowed down on my sandwich, which was super-delicious, with orange cheese and mayonnaise. I felt bad that she had to eat that nasty green stuff.

"Want my Jell-O, Gabrielle?" I asked, even though it was a little hard to let it go. I love red Jell-O, but I knew she would really like it too.

"Really? I've never had Jell-O before."

"You're kidding!" I nearly shouted. "Everyone eats Jell-O."

"Not me," she said. "I have always wanted to try,

but I'm not allowed."

"Wow!" I said, still in shock.

"Thank you so very much," she said as she dug right in and scooped a wiggly spoonful. "Mmm . . . that is so good!"

"I know! You should try the purple one too! It's grape flavored."

"Refried Bean and Goony Gaby sitting in a tree!" Terrible Tanisha said as she threw a balled-up dirty napkin right at us.

I don't know what I was thinking being friends with that girl. She is m-e-a-n MEAN! I ignored her because I was way too busy telling Gabrielle about all the yummy flavors of Jell-O and all the other sweet and sugary bad stuff she just had to try! Afterward, we threw out our trash and skipped back to the classroom chatting the whole way about Cheetos, Sour Snakes, Slurpees, and cookie dough.

In the afternoon, Ms. Sullivan took us to the computer lab. I chose a computer all the way in the last row, next to Gabrielle. I was about to open up the word games, which are my favorite, when I had a great idea! I decided to send Carla an "I'm sorry" email!

To: Carlacat@mailman.com

From: LilBean@mailman.com

Subject: Im sooooooooo soory.

Carla--

Im so sorry u got hurt. It was not me tho. Tanisha is mean and pushed the door and blamed me. Im sorry. Dont b mad at me.

Bean :)

I watched Carla from the corner of my eye to see if she had read my email yet, and while I waited and waited, I went back to playing word games, making words from letters floating across the screen. Sure enough, after a couple minutes, Carla turned around in her seat and stared right at me. She must have read my email. I smiled my biggest "I'm so-o-o-o-o-o sorry" smile and I thought she smiled back. I mean it was kinda a smile, like a half smile.

When the bell rang for the end of the day, we

grabbed our backpacks, lined up, and headed out to the playground. I couldn't go home yet, though, since Rose had to stay after school. While Gardenia ran around with her friends, I just sat and leaned against the fence with my eyes closed.

It was fun when me and Carla used to play after school. We would act like monkeys and try to swing all the way across the jungle gym without touching the ground. My hands would burn and my arms would ache, but we still had so much fun because we were together.

I snapped out of my daydream when a basketball bounced between my legs. I opened my eyes. Sam was standing right above me.

"Um . . . hi," I said, holding the ball. She just stood there with a sort of angry, give-me-my-ball-back kinda look, so I continued, "I didn't do it, you know. It was Tanisha and I feel really bad. I would never hurt Carla. Never!"

"I know," she finally said, softening her glare. "Tanisha is so mean."

"I don't know what I was thinking hanging out

with her," I said. I threw the ball back to Sam.

She caught it easily and started dribbling it with her left hand. Then she switched to her right hand mindlessly, like she was thinking something over before answering me. Finally, she said, "Do you wanna shoot some hoops?"

"Really?" I asked. "You're not angry at me?"

"I was mad, but I believe you, Bean. I know you would never do something that mean. That's the work of Tanisha for sure." Sam threw me the ball. "So, you wanna play or not?"

"Okay," I agreed, of course.

I dribbled the best I could, which was not very good at all. I had to use two hands instead of one and stare right at the ball. I threw it back to her and we ran over to the hoop.

"Let's play Pig," she suggested.

Pig is a fun game! Here is how you play: One person shoots the basketball, and if she gets it in the hoop, then the other person has to stand in the exact same spot and try to get it in too. If she misses the shot, then she gets a *P*. If she misses it again, she gets an *I* and then a *G* and then you lose because P-I-G spells pig, you know.

Sam got her first two shots in, but I missed mine, of course. I've never been too good at basketball. Then Sam did a layup and got another one in. I ran and leaped just like she did, but my ball swirled around the rim and fell to the side. I got PIG pretty quick, but I didn't care. It was still fun to play.

We shot hoops till Sam's big brother, Marcus, came to get her. Marcus is in middle school with Rose. He is so cute! His skin is like caramel. He's tall and has perfectly cornrowed hair. His eyes are the most gorgeous shade of green, and even though I h-a-t-e HATE the color green, I like it in Marcus's eyeballs. I don't have a crush on him or anything. . . . Okay, well, maybe just a little.

"Hey, little Bean," Marcus said with a wink.

"Hi," I said, trying to stay calm while pretending that butterflies weren't going crazy in my tummy. Rose came up, and I could tell she had butterflies too.

"Oh, hey, Marcus," she said.

"Hi, Rose," he said as he motioned for Sam to follow him. "See you guys later."

"Yeah. Sure. Yes. That would be great," Rose said.

"See ya tomorrow, Sam!" I shouted behind them.

"See ya!" Sam called over her shoulder.

"Rose has a boyfriend! Rose has a boyfriend!" Gardenia ran up, singing, when Sam and Marcus were gone. She didn't stop teasing Rose the whole way home.

When we walked in the door, I gave Dad a squeeze.

"How was today?" he asked.

"I didn't get in any trouble," I said, and then I headed straight up to my room without even being told. I was gonna be a good girl from now on, for sure!

I finished my homework and practiced my violin all before dinnertime. After dinner, I practiced some more. I was getting much better at the violin. Dad said he would teach me the song "Twinkle Twinkle" to play at the recital, which was great because I already know how it goes.

When Mom got home from work, she came and tucked me in. "Dad said you did well today."

"Yep," I let her know. "And I'm gonna be good from now on."

"I like the sound of that!" she said as she turned out the lights.

Even though Carla still wasn't my friend, I felt like everything was getting a little bit better. It was fun playing with Sam after school and I liked having lunch with Gabrielle and Ms. Sullivan didn't hate me anymore and I was getting excited about the recital and . . . *zzzz*. . . .

13

Black-and-Blue

The next day during recess, I was sitting on the bench with Gabrielle. We were just swinging our feet and watching Sam, Carla, and some of the boys running around, when—guess what? Sam asked us if we wanted to play with them.

Gabrielle said, "No, thank you," of course, because she never plays at recess, but I agreed . . . even though Carla gave me a dirty look.

"Let's play dodgeball," Sam suggested.

I didn't want to be the target for balls being

thrown a million miles an hour, particularly coming from Carla, who still hadn't forgiven me, but I helped gather balls anyway.

John drew a long white line with chalk across the cement, and then we counted off. One, two, one, two, one . . .

"Two," I said, which put me on a team with Jerry, John, and Carla, who did not look happy to be on my team.

"Okay, go!" John yelled at the top of his lungs, and balls started flying through the air.

I grabbed a big red ball and tossed it at Mark, but it just bounced in front of him.

"Ha-ha!" he laughed as he picked it up and threw it at me. I tried to jump out of the way, but it slammed me right on the leg. *Oww!*

Since I had gotten hit, I was out. I had to sit on the sidelines and wait for someone on my team to catch a ball. I rubbed my leg while I waited. It was gonna turn black and blue, for sure.

I think Carla dropped a ball on purpose so I would have to stay out of the game. But Jerry finally caught one and called, "Bean, you're in!"

Just as I hobbled back to the game, a ball flew past my ear, missing me by a hair. I grabbed another one and hurled it as hard as I could. I hit Sam right in the knee. "*Yes!*" I shouted as I jumped in the air, but as I came down, a ball slammed me right in the side of my head. *OUCH!*

I trudged over and sat on the sidelines again.

John caught a ball right away. I didn't want to play anymore, but I dragged myself into the game. When I got to my spot, Mark, who is the tallest and strongest boy in the class, pulled back his arm like a slingshot, and the huge, black ball was pointed right at me! I closed my eyes and covered my head to protect it, but luckily I was saved by the bell, which rang just before I would have gotten clobbered.

"Good game," everyone said as they high-fived, but not Carla.

I went back and grabbed Gabrielle and headed into the building

When we got to the classroom, Ms. Sullivan said, "We are going to do a fun math project today."

I like when we do cool projects instead of just solving problems and equations in our workbooks. Ms. Sullivan explained that we were going to glue macaroni to a piece of construction paper to show the six multiplication table. Then she broke everyone up into groups of two and—guess what? Ms. Sullivan put me with Sam.

"But Sam and I are always partners," Carla whined.

"I know," Ms. Sullivan said. "Sometimes it's good to work with someone else to get a new perspective on things."

Carla slumped down in her seat. She got paired up with Gabrielle, which is actually pretty good, because not only is Gabrielle a goody-two-shoes, she is also a smarty-pants.

Me and Sam were a good team, because I am good at multiplication tables and she is really good at gluing macaroni.

On Friday, I spotted Sam hanging out on the playground after school, alone again.

"Where's Carla?" I asked.

"Her mom picked her up. She had a dentist appointment."

"Oh," I said. "I hate the dentist."

"Me too."

"Hey, maybe do you want to come over my house and play?"

"Are you sure? Your sister told my brother you were grounded," she said.

"Not anymore," I said. And boy, was I happy the week of being stuck in my room was over.

"Okay, then, I just have to ask my brother."

When Marcus walked up, Rose was skipping along right beside him. She was giggling and I could tell she was in l-o-v-e LOVE!

"Hey, Marcus, can I go over to Bean's to play?" asked Sam.

"Maybe you could come by too," Rose said with a flip of her hair. "My birthday's tomorrow, and some of my friends are going to Joey's Pizza tonight to celebrate."

"I guess that would be cool," Marcus said.

On the way home, Rose and Marcus trailed way

behind, and she totally forgot to hold my hand when we crossed the street. I know the rules, though, so I held on to Sam instead.

When we got home, Rose, Gardenia, Marcus, and Mom all left for Joey's Pizza to meet up with Rose's friends. Dad stayed home with me and Sam.

"Wait here," I said to Sam. I ran as fast as I could up to my room and grabbed all my dolls and Barbies and shoveled them under the bed. I didn't want her to think I was a baby or anything. Then I rushed back downstairs.

"Wanna go play in my room?"

"Sure," she said, and followed me.

We bounced on my bed and laughed as we threw the pillows in the air. Then Sam had a great idea. She said, "Let's build a fort!"

We yanked all the pillows and blankets off the beds, making a huge pile in the middle of the room. I ran to the linen closet and got more pillows and sheets and comforters.

"Stand the pillows up like this," said Sam. She leaned the big ones against the bed to make walls.

I spread the sheets across the top to make the roof. We kept building and building until the fort was so big, it filled up the whole room.

I got down on my hands and knees and crawled through the halls of the fort. Sam followed.

"What's this?" she asked as she held my doll Cindy by her leg in front of my face. "You play with dolls?"

"No . . . um . . . not anymore . . . um . . . not really," I stuttered. "Those are old."

"Dolls are for babies."

"I know," I said with a laugh.

"Dinnertime, girls," Dad called from downstairs.

We both stood up and broke through the ceiling of the fort. The walls of pillows and sheets crumpled around us. We climbed out of the mess and headed downstairs.

Dad had ordered a pizza for us. It was fun having the whole table to ourselves and the whole yummy cheesy pizza too.

Just as we finished dinner, everyone burst through the door and into the living room. Rose and all her friends were n-o-i-s-y NOISY, but they looked like they were having a lot of fun. I want to have my next birthday party at Joey's too, but I have to wait till summertime because my birthday is in June, you know.

Marcus said good-bye to everyone, then came into the kitchen to get Sam.

"We gotta get home," he said.

"That was fun, Bean," said Sam with a wave. "Thanks."

"See you Monday."

Once Sam was gone, Dad said, "Why don't you go clean up and get ready for bed?"

"But I don't want to go to bed. I want to hang out with Rose."

"Rose wants to be alone with her friends tonight, and it's almost bedtime anyway."

"Fine." I marched right by Rose and all her friends, who were still giggling about Marcus and how cute he is.

What a mess! I had forgotten about the flattened fort all over the floor.

I spent what felt like hours trying to make the beds and folding the sheets, which was hard to do by myself. When I was all finished, I plopped down on my bed without even brushing my teeth or washing my face. I know it's important to wash up before bedtime, but I was exhausted. I was fast asleep even before Mom came to tuck me in and turn out the lights.

School wasn't so bad now that I had a few friends. Me and Gabrielle sat together every day at lunch and—guess what? She likes Cheetos and Jell-O and snickerdoodles just as much as I do now. She had never had them before, but I was teaching her all about good food. She shared her apple slices too, and even though they are healthy, I thought they were yummy.

Sam and I were friends too, even though it made Carla m-a-d MAD! Life is so much better when you don't have to eat all by yourself or stand alone in line and when you have people to play with at recess.

One afternoon, a big kid named Donald

suggested we play freeze tag. I like tag because I can run pretty fast and no one is throwing things at you.

"You're It!" yelled Sam as she tapped my shoulder.

The whole group scattered. Jerry ran behind the tree. Donald ran to the fence and Sam took off toward the jungle gym, followed by Carla. I ran as fast as I could. I chased Sam around the jungle gym but missed her. Then I followed Jerry to the tree.

"Gotcha!" I yelled. I tagged him and he froze like a statue.

I caught everyone except Carla, because I was too scared to get close to her. Next, Donald was It. I ran as fast as my legs would go to the fence. He's big and kinda chubby, so he was really slow. When he got close, I took off and ran around the jungle gym.

"You can't catch me!" I teased.

I waited till he got close and then I bolted again. I ran circles around him, which made Sam laugh. I was having so much fun that I didn't pay attention to how angry Donald was getting.

"You're a slowpoke! Slowpoke!" I sang.

I guess my joking around made my feet slow down so much that Donald caught up. He shoved me with all his might.

I flew forward, tumbled like a rag doll, and skidded across the cement. Everything hurt, but I couldn't see the damage because my glasses had fallen off. I scrambled to find them, and as I slid them back on my nose, I saw that I had scraped my knees so bad that the knee parts of my jeans had ripped. There were bloody scratches underneath, and my palms were all cut up too.

I've gotten pretty tough, so I could take all of that, but my finger really, really hurt. It was throbbing and getting swollen like a balloon. It wouldn't even move or bend.

"Are you okay, Bean?" asked Sam.

"Yeah, I'm fine," I lied. I didn't want her to think I was a crybaby.

"Sorry," said Donald. "I didn't mean to push you so hard."

"It's okay," I said.

"Come on," said Jerry. "Let's go play basketball."

And just like that, the boys marched off toward the hoop at the other side of the playground.

"You guys go ahead without me," I called after them with a wave of my bloody hand.

"You sure you're okay?" Sam asked again.

"Yeah. Sure. I'll be over in a second," I said, trying to keep the tears from filling my eyes.

"Okay," she said, but when she left, I started to cry. And not a little-drippy-tear-down-your-cheek kinda cry. I let out huge sobs with buckets of tears. I dropped to my knees and curled up into a little ball and kept crying and crying.

"Are you okay?" a voice asked.

I looked up and it was Carla.

"No, I think I'm really hurt," I said through my tears and runny nose and bloody knees and hands.

"Come on," she said, and she helped me up.

We walked to the nurse's office without saying even a word.

"Bean, what happened?" asked Nurse Beth.

"I fell and skinned my knees and my hands and my finger hurts bad."

She cleaned off my knees and hands with hydrogen peroxide. It stung a little, but it looked cool when it bubbled up all white and frothy. Next, she looked closely at my finger.

"I think we'd better call your parents so they can have a doctor check it out," she said.

Now I started to worry. I must have really hurt it if my parents were being called in. I slumped over in my chair as Nurse Beth left the room to use the phone. Carla came and sat next to me.

"Remember when we were playing hide-and-seek and your sister pushed me and then you pushed her back?"

"Yeah! Gardenia got so mad."

"Yeah, and then we made up that song while we sat on your back stoop."

"Oh, yeah!" I said with a smile. "Do you remember the words?"

"I sure do," she said.

We both started singing. "Friends forever. La-di-da-di-dee. Fighting never. La-di-da-di-do. We are so clever. La-di-da-di-dee."

"I'm so sorry, Carla," I said. My tears started to fall again. "I'm sorry I didn't keep in touch over the summer."

"I'm sorry too. I was really mean," Carla said. She gave me a big hug.

Everything still hurt, but right at that moment I felt just fine.

14

Worse Than Ever

I swung my feet back and forth as I sat next to Carla in the office. Sam and Gabrielle came to check on me too.

"Do you think it's broken?" asked Carla.

"Once I broke my arm. I went to the hospital and they x-rayed it," Sam said. "I could see all my bones."

"Oh, dear," Gabrielle gasped. "Luckily, I have never broken anything,"

Just then, Mom came flying through the door and I waved with my cut-up hand.

"Are you all right?" she asked.

"Yeah, I'm okay," I said with a smile.

"Hello, everyone," said Mom. "It's so nice to see you, Carla."

"You too, Mrs. Gibson."

"Now, let's check you out, Bean," Mom said as she looked closely at my finger and moved it around gently. *Ouch!*

"It does look broken, honey."

"Really?" I said. Then I added, "Can I get it x-rayed, so I can see all my bones?"

"You don't usually need an X-ray for a finger, but I guess we could stop by the hospital on the way home. We can also pick up a splint while we're there."

"Hello, Mrs. Gibson. My name is Gabrielle." Gabrielle gave Mom's hand a polite shake. "I was wondering if you might tell me what a splint is?"

"It's very nice to meet you, Gabrielle," Mom said. Then she explained, "A splint is something that will hold the finger still, so it doesn't move around."

"I had a cast on my arm once and everyone signed it and drew pictures," Sam said.

"Well, Sam, it's kind of like that, but much smaller, just for your finger." Mom headed toward the door. "Come on, Bean. Let's go."

"Feel better," Carla said.

"Thanks, Carla," I said.

"Bye, Bean," Sam and Gabrielle called before the door closed behind us.

"Looks like Carla and you have worked things out," Mom said as we headed to the car. "And Gabrielle seems nice too."

"Yep, things are getting much better." I hopped in and buckled up.

It was pretty cool to have some alone time with Mom. I didn't have to fight for a seat, I could talk about whatever I wanted, and I even got to pick the radio station.

Mom parked the car in the employee parking garage at the hospital. We headed right in through the sliding doors. I think it's supercool how the doors know when you're coming and open up all by themselves. I walked in and out and in and out. Open. Close. Op—

"Okay Bean, that's enough. Let's go."

I walked through one more time and then followed Mom up the stairs to the second floor. She waved at a man with a shiny bald head standing by the desk in the middle of the room. He was wearing blue scrubs just like hers.

"Hey, Jason, could you do me a favor and x-ray my daughter's hand?"

"All righty," said Jason with a warm smile.

He led me into a room with a big cameralike machine. He told me to put my hand flat on the cold surface and then he covered me with a thick bluish-silver blanket. It was heavy and not soft at all. He said it was to protect my insides. I wondered why my hand didn't need protection too.

"I'll be right behind that wall," he said. "Stay very still."

I sat like a statue and held my breath while Jason slid behind the wall. I could see him pull a lever, which made the lights flash and a buzzer ring. He came inside and gently flipped my hand over and did it all again, then led me back out into the hall where Mom was waiting.

"She did really well," Jason told Mom.

Mom and I waited in the hallway while the X-rays developed like film from one of those disposable cameras. The hall was bright white and clean and it smelled like medicine. A guy rolled by in a wheelchair. He was all bandaged up, and he moaned like he hurt all over. Poor thing! Boy, was I glad I only hurt my finger and not my whole body.

Jason finally returned with two big pictures of the bones in my hand, only they didn't look like my hand at all. They looked like a spooky skeleton hand.

"Look"—Mom pointed to one of the fingers on the X-ray—"see how it's broken right there?"

I got really close and squinted, but it was hard to tell. I believed her, though, because she's a nurse and also because my finger was killing me.

"Thanks, Jason," Mom said. We headed back down the stairs and into the waiting room. "Sit here, Bean. I'm going to get a splint from the supply room."

Mom disappeared down the hall. I thought

about Carla and smiled to myself, but then my happy thoughts were interrupted. The man sitting next to me was as big as a bear and coughing like he was about to throw up his insides. *Yuck!* I covered my face with my sleeve, so I wouldn't breathe his nasty germs.

I looked around, and everyone in the waiting room looked s-i-c-k SICK! I could feel the germs like cooties all over my body. I wiggled in my seat and covered my whole head with my sweatshirt, but I couldn't take it anymore! No open, close, open, close of the door this time. I jumped up and rushed right through the hospital door.

Right as I stepped outside, an ambulance pulled up. It screeched to a stop and the doors flew open. I rushed to the side to get out of the way of the EMTs. That means ambulance drivers, you know. They worked fast as they pulled a lady lying flat on a board from the ambulance. She was tied down with red straps and had all sorts of tubes sticking out of her.

I hoped and hoped that she was going to be okay

as they swooped past me and disappeared into the hospital. Right then and there, I decided that maybe I want to be an EMT when I grow up, so I can save people when they are in really bad shape.

"Oh, my goodness, Bean," said Mom as she came through the door. "I was looking for you everywhere. I told you to stay put."

"I know, but there were so many germs and coughing and sick people. I had to leave," I said.

I don't know how Mom deals with all that yucky sickness every day.

"Okay," Mom said. "Let's get this splint on your finger and go home."

Mom knelt down in front of me and bent the metal splint around my palm. Then she strapped my finger down tight with two white strips of tape. It hurt at first, but then it just felt kinda funny. Usually, my finger moves all around, but now it was stuck pointing straight up.

"Look over there." I pointed my splinted finger toward the street.

"What is it?" Mom asked.

"Nothing—it's just that my finger is always pointing to something now."

As we drove back home, we laughed over and over again as I kept pointing at things I didn't mean to.

"Maybe I'll have everyone sign my splint," I said as we pulled into the driveway.

"Don't you think it's too small for everyone's names?"

"Yeah, but maybe everyone can put their initials on the tape," I said. "*C* for Carla, then *S* for Sam and *G* for Gabrielle."

When we got home, my sisters were already back from school.

"What happened?" asked Rose as she rushed over and gave me a hug.

"I fell during recess and broke my finger. Look!" I said as I held up my hand.

"Does it hurt?" Gardenia asked, leaning in to get a better look.

"It did, but it's not so bad anymore."

"I'm glad you are all right," Dad said as he gave

me a good, long I'm-happy-you-are-okay kinda squeeze.

Mom got started on dinner. Dad, Rose, and Gardenia went into the living room to practice their instruments, and I started my homework at the kitchen table.

All I had was cursive homework, which usually takes no time at all. This time, when I tried to write with my pencil, my finger just stuck straight out. It was hard to grab the pencil without a pointer finger to hold it. I struggled to trace the *M*'s and *N*'s, and then with no dots to follow, it was a mess. Even though it took like what seemed like forever, I finally finished and had time to check my email before dinner, and—guess what? There was an email from Tanya!

To: LilBean@mailman.com

From: TTBaby@mailman.com

Subject: Miss u!

Hey B.

Sorry Ive been so MIA. Computer broke and lotsa work at school. Hope things get better 4 u. How r

things w/Carla? You makin new friends? I have a friend named Donna. Shes soooo funny. Ud love her!

Hope 2 see u soon.

T

I was so happy to hear from her. I missed her a whole bunch and I had so much to tell her. Typing wasn't too bad with a broken finger because I only use two fingers anyway, so I emailed her right back.

To: TTBaby@mailman.com

From: LilBean@mailman.com

Subject: Re: Miss u!

Guess what? I broke my finger 2day and went 2 hospital and got 2 c my bones in an xray. Carla and me r friends again and now I have other friends 2. Im learnin violin and gettin kinda good, u no. Im gonna be in a perfomenc soon.

TTYL

Bean

"Dinnertime," Mom called just as I logged off.

I skipped into the kitchen feeling g-o-o-d GOOD. I hopped right into my seat, flipped my napkin in my lap, and swung my legs to the tune I was humming. Mom scooped some chicken and potatoes and peas onto my plate and boy, did it smell yummy. But, when it was time to dig in, my happy mood turned m-a-d MAD. It was so hard to hold that stinkin' fork!

Gardenia kept laughing like a hyena every time peas dropped all over my lap. Rose laughed when my chicken fell off my plate, and Mom and Dad laughed too. I didn't think it was very funny at all. . . . Okay, maybe just a little.

After dinner, the worst thing of all happened. I pulled out my violin to practice, but I couldn't even hold the stupid bow with my dumb, broken finger. It hurt really bad when I pushed down on the strings with the bow, so all I could make was sick-cat, screechy sounds, instead of the good "Twinkle Twinkle" sounds that I had learned. Just when I thought I was starting to sound pretty good, I was worse than ever.

15

No Practice Makes Not Perfect

Before I knew it, Thanksgiving was here. I love Thanksgiving because I love turkey and stuffing and sweet potato pie and I love, love, love that I don't have to go to school.

My finger still had the splint on, so luckily, my sweet potatoes stuck to the fork and no one yelled at me when I ate my turkey with my fingers. I left my greens and cranberries right on my plate because I knew they were gonna be slippery. Well, also because cranberries are icky and greens are yucky.

On Friday, Dad wanted me to practice, but it was too hard to hold the bow with the splint on my finger. I didn't care though, because someone was knocking at the door—and I knew just who it was.

"Carla!"

"Hey, Bean." Carla greeted me with a big, warm best-friend kinda hug. "How was Thanksgiving dinner?"

"Delicious!" I licked my lips.

Sam was at the door too. Did you know that having lots of friends is even better than just having one best friend? When Carla can't talk on the phone because she has to finish her homework, I have a whole bunch of other friends I can call. And when I need help climbing the fence on the playground, I have more hands to give me a boost.

"Wanna go to 7-Eleven and share a Slurpee? I've got two dollars," Sam suggested, and you know, I love Slurpees. I grabbed my jacket and we marched right out the back door and down the stairs.

We passed by Rose and Gardenia, who were playing hopscotch outside.

"Where are you guys going?" Gardenia yelled in my direction. I just ignored her, like she always does to me. I have my own friends now.

We walked past the line of garbage cans. Black is for trash, blue for things that can be recycled, like Coke cans and cardboard boxes, and green is for . . .

"What's the green garbage can for?" I asked.

"Boogers!" Carla laughed as she grabbed me with tickling fingers.

"Ha-ha!" I broke free, and we ran down the block, around the corner, and all the way to 7-Eleven.

We pushed through the door, and I said hi to Darnell, who is big and wide and shaped like an Easter egg. He smiled at us, showing his teeth that look like marshmallows, big and white against his dark skin.

"Hey, there, kids," he said with a wave. The skin on his arm wiggled and jiggled back and forth. I had never even seen him leave that seat behind the counter. I wondered if it was hard for Darnell to move around.

"What flavor should we get?" Sam asked. We

stared at all the different-color nozzles.

"Blue raspberry is our favorite," I said quickly, but then remembered that Carla had changed her mind. "I mean it's my favorite."

"Blue raspberry is still my favorite," Carla said, "but I like green apple too."

I scrunched up my nose because I h-a-t-e HATE the color green, you know.

"I have an idea," Sam said.

"What?" Carla and I said at the very same time.

"Let's mix them together." She smiled a big aren't-I-smart? kinda smile.

I guess it was a good idea. I mean if you mixed them together, they wouldn't be green anymore, and raspberry apple did sound yummy.

"Let's do it," I said, and Carla agreed.

I chose a medium cup because that was the size we could afford. It was hard to hold it with my broken finger, so I passed it to Carla, who held it steady under the hole. I pulled the blue raspberry nozzle, and when the cup was half full, I moved to the side so Sam could fill the rest with green apple.

We each grabbed a straw and swizzled them around until the blue and green mixed and made a yummy greenish-bluish color, kinda like the ocean. We all leaned in and took a long slurp from our straws. Oh! Brain freeze! I gripped my head and scrunched my eyes closed.

"What's wrong with you?" a familiar voice defrosted my brain.

I peeked though one eye, hoping it wasn't who I thought it was, but sure enough, Terrible Tanisha was standing there right in front of me with a bag of Cheetos swinging from her fingers.

"Oh, hey," I said. "Um . . . I drank too fast and froze my brain."

"I hate when that happens," Tanisha said. She spotted Sam and Carla, who were hiding behind the lollipops. "What're you guys doing?"

"Just hanging out."

"Oh." Tanisha looked sad.

I couldn't help feeling bad for her. I mean I know from experience that being lonely is no fun at all. Plus it was Thanksgiving vacation, which is a time to help others . . . at least that's what Mom said last year when she made us serve sandwiches, not soup, at the soup kitchen to people with no house to live in and no food to eat.

Since we hadn't gone to the soup kitchen this year and I hadn't helped anyone yet, I asked Tanisha, "Wanna play with us?"

First Tanisha just stared at me. It wasn't a yes or a no. It was more of a blank, I'm-thinking kinda stare. Then she barked, "I ain't some charity case, loser. Get out of my way."

I'm not sure what she meant. I was only trying to be nice, but I guess Tanisha didn't like *nice.* She pushed past us, leaving her Cheetos behind and knocking right into Carla.

"Oww," Carla moaned, and rubbed her shoulder.

"Are you okay?" Sam asked.

"I'm fine, but I don't like that girl at all."

"Why is she so mean?" Sam asked.

"I think she's just lonely," I said. "She has no one to play with, you know."

"Well, maybe if she wasn't so nasty, someone

would want to play with her," Carla said.

That's for sure, I thought.

We walked to the counter, where Sam paid Darnell for the Slurpee. Then we pushed the swinging door and walked down the block and around the corner, passing the Slurpee among us the whole way. Mmm . . . raspberry apple is my new favorite flavor!

When we got back home, we sat on the stoop and finished the last sips.

"What should we do now?" Carla asked.

"Wanna play hopscotch?" I suggested, since my sisters had left perfectly good boxes and numbers drawn in chalk on the driveway.

We got a pebble and hopped and skipped, till Sam made it all the way to the end. She won because me and Carla were still on 6. Next, we played hide-and-seek, and I found the best spot—under the back stairs by the garage. But then I saw a hairy, nasty spider and I screamed, so of course I got caught.

We had played for a long time and the sun was now behind the trees.

"I better head home before it gets dark," Sam said.

"I guess I should go too," said Carla.

Sam and Carla walked down the block and out of sight. My heart felt happy and full. Just as I was about to head into the house, Mom's car pulled up in the driveway.

"Hey, Bean," she said, getting out of the car. "Did you have a good day?"

"Yep, I sure did."

"Well, I know something that's going to make it even better."

"Really! What?"

"It's time to take that splint off your finger."

Yippee!

"I am sure it's all healed by now."

"Oh, I hope so!"

We headed into the kitchen and Mom carefully cut the tape, just like she had been doing every couple of days. You have to change the tape, you know, or it will get dirty and stinky and infected. This time, though, she removed the metal splint too.

"Try and move your finger," she said.

It felt a little stiff and it looked all wrinkly and skinny, but—guess what? It worked just fine.

I could hold a fork without dropping stuff and even write in cursive. Well, sort of. I mean, my *M*'s sometimes had three bumps instead of two and my *J*'s still looked more like *G*'s, but I was getting better.

I ran right past Dad in the living room. I gave him a quick wave, but then I headed straight upstairs to get my violin. I wanted to try to play with my new fixed finger.

I brought the case to the living room, unlatched it, and grabbed the bow. My finger didn't hurt at all! Then I set the violin on my shoulder, put my fingers on the strings, placed the bow, and pulled. My finger was just fine, but you know how they say practice makes perfect . . . Well, no practice makes . . . *screech!*

Dad said, "Sounds like that needs some work."

"I'll never be good enough."

"Yes, you will. It's time for you to start believing in yourself."

I smiled, but I was still scared.

"Look who's here," Dad said with a smile.

"Hey." Stanley appeared from the kitchen.

"Hey," I said back.

"Bean's feeling a little down about her violin. Maybe you two can play together?" Dad suggested.

I sighed and slumped over my violin.

"Sounds good," Stanley said. "How was your holiday?"

"Good."

"When did you get your splint off?" he asked

"Today," I said. I knew I should answer with more than one word, but I just wasn't feeling happy, you know.

"Cool. Well, should we get started?"

"Oh, all right," I said, and even though I didn't want to, I started to play . . . *screech!*

"I'm not gonna play in the stinkin' performance."

"Just keep trying, Bean," Stanley said.

"No way!"

"Come on. It'll get better."

"Okay," I finally agreed, because I knew he was

gonna keep bugging me till I tried again.

We played scales over and over again. We played and played and played until it got completely dark outside, and then we kept playing some more. Playing with Stanley was actually superfun. He plays really good and he is also pretty funny. He played his song for the performance standing on one foot with a sheet on his head, and I played mine from inside the closet wearing Gardenia's gorilla mask from Halloween. With all the playing, I was starting to get better at holding the bow, and my notes didn't sound so terrible . . . but it still was not good enough.

"Stanley, your mom's here," Dad called.

"I gotta go, but maybe I can come over tomorrow and we can play some more," Stanley said as he packed up his saxophone.

"Thanks, Stanley. That would be great."

When Mom came to tuck me in that night, she had a great idea.

"I was thinking maybe it would be nice if we invited Tanya to the performance," Mom suggested. "Would you like that?"

"Yeah. That would be great."

"I'll call and invite her. Grand Mommy and Aunt Bobbie too."

"Could Carla and Sam come?" I asked.

"Sure, you can invite anyone you want."

She gave me a kiss on the forehead, which usually calms my mind and helps me fall asleep, but not tonight. My brain was filled with fears about the performance. What if I couldn't make the notes? What if I tripped and fell off the stage? What if everyone laughed at me and booed?

16

The Big Day

The day of the performance was finally here. I had all these twisty-turny feelings in my tummy. I wiggled my arm from under the covers and grabbed my glasses. I pushed them up on my nose and peeked around the room.

Gardenia was still fast asleep. *Shhh* . . . I slid slowly out of my bed and onto the floor. Maybe I could hide under my bed till it was too late to go to school. I needed more time to practice.

The problem was, there was not much room

under there, with all the dolls and stuffed animals, dirty clothes, and old, torn-up shoes. I made myself small like a ball, so every bit of me would be hidden.

I could hear Mom walking in the hall, and then her sneakers came into the room and right up to my bed. I held my breath.

"Wake up, girls," Mom said, as she gently shook Gardenia and moved the covers around on my bed.

"Bean, where are you?"

I couldn't hold my breath for one second longer or I would've passed out for sure. All the air in my lungs came shooting from of my mouth. It made Mom's shoelaces blow in the wind.

"Bean"—she stuck her head under the bed to see me—"what are you doing?"

"I can't go to school today. I won't go. I have to practice. There is so much to do!"

"After school you will have plenty of time to get ready," she said as she pulled me by my foot. "The performance is not till tonight."

I tried to hold on to the leg of the bed, but it was no use. I lost my grip, and she dragged me like a sack of potatoes to the middle of the room.

"Now get ready so you girls won't be late."

"Mom, can I take my violin to school so that I can practice?"

"When will you have time to play?"

I thought and thought and then said, "Maybe at lunchtime or recess."

"I don't see why not, as long as Ms. Sullivan doesn't mind."

"And, Mom, you promise to be there tonight, right?" I asked.

"Of course, baby. I wouldn't miss it for the world."

"But what if there are triplets born at the hospital today or quadruplets?"

"Even if there are octuplets," she said with a laugh. "Baby, I know I've gotten stuck at work before and missed important things, but I promise I'll make it tonight."

I gave Mom a good, long hug around her middle.

"I promise," she whispered in my ear.

A promise is like a pinky-swear that you can't break. I felt much better now. I scurried to the bathroom and got ready.

At school, I couldn't concentrate at all. My math was a mess of musical notes instead of numbers, and during cursive, instead of writing out my spelling words, I wrote the words to my song, "Twinkle Twinkle Little Star." Then the bell rang for recess. I dragged my feet when it was time to line up with the class.

"What's going on, Bean?" Ms. Sullivan asked. "You seem a little down today."

"I'm okay," I said. "I'm just nervous because I'm playing my violin in the big holiday performance tonight at the college where my dad teaches."

"Oh, that's very exciting."

"Yeah, I guess," I said with a shrug. "I'm just scared that I'm gonna be bad, you know."

"If you'd like, you can stay in the classroom during recess and practice."

"Really? That would be great! Can Carla and Sam stay too?"

"Yes," Ms. Sullivan said. "That would be fine."

I spotted Stanley in the front of the line and

asked, "Stanley, could you stay too?"

Carla and Sam stared at me wide-eyed, but I know that Stanley is a great help when you're feeling scared about playing the violin.

"Sure," he said.

The whole class headed out to the playground except me, Carla, Sam, and Stanley. I moved to the front of the room and opened up my violin case.

Sam pretended to be the announcer and said, "And now, put your hands together for Bean playing the violin!"

Carla and Stanley clapped as I strutted to the front of the room. I put my violin on my shoulder, placed the bow on the strings and—

"Excuse me," Gabrielle said as she pushed through the classroom door. "Is Ms. Sullivan here?"

"Nope," Carla said.

"What are you guys doing?" Gabrielle asked.

"Practicing for my performance. I'm going to play the violin tonight at the college."

I had a feeling Gabrielle wasn't really looking for Ms. Sullivan. She probably just wanted to come hang out with us, so I asked her if she wanted to stay and listen too.

"That would be wonderful," Gabrielle said.

"Please take your seat," Sam said to Gabrielle. Then she announced into an eraser from the chalkboard, like it was a microphone, "Prepare yourself for a spectacular performance by Bean Gibson!"

I stood up tall, with my head held high, in the front of the classroom. I took a deep breath and started to play, and—guess what? I played better than I ever had in my whole life! The notes were strong and loud and not even the littlest bit squeaky. My friends cheered as I took a bow, then a curtsy, and then one more bow for effect.

"Stanley is playing in the performance too, and Carla and Sam are coming to watch. Do you want to come?" I asked Gabrielle.

"I would absolutely love to, but I will have to ask my mother," Gabrielle said, with a tiny bit of a grimace. I know her mom is tough, so I wasn't sure she would make it.

"What are you gonna wear?" Gabrielle asked.

"Hmm . . . I don't know."

"Well, you can't wear those holey jeans," she said.

I looked down and she was right. I wanted to wear something special, but I hadn't really thought about what I was gonna wear. Mom had laid out my church dress, but I'd worn it so many times, it wasn't really all that special.

"Would you like to borrow one of my dresses?" Gabrielle asked.

I thought about how pretty I would look in one of her frilly dresses, standing on the stage. "I would love, love, love to!"

"I'll bring my very prettiest dress by your house after school," she said with a smile. All of Gabrielle's dresses are so pretty, so I couldn't wait to see the prettiest one!

The rest of the day, my mind kept wandering. I was able to focus a little during reading, but only because I really like the book we're reading, *Charlotte's Web*. Then during art, instead of painting the bowl of fruit, I painted the sky with twinkly little stars.

The minute the bell rang, I ran out to the

playground to find my sisters. We met up quickly. They were excited about the performance too, so we rushed right home. We busted through the door and raced up the stairs. Rose made it to the shower first and then blow-dried her hair till it was straight and long. Gardenia was next, and she took what felt like forever in the shower.

"Hurry up in there!" I yelled through the shower curtain. The steam fogged up my glasses.

"Relax!" she yelled back. "There's plenty of time."

I sat on the toilet seat, tapping my foot and staring at the clock. Now I would never have enough time to get ready!

The minute Gardenia got out of the shower, I hopped right in and got to washing my hair. I sang under the sprinkle of warm water, "Twinkle twinkle little star, How I wonder what you are, up above the world so high, Like a diamond in the sky—"

"Thank God you're not singing in the performance tonight!" Gardenia yelled.

I peeked around the curtain to stick my tongue out at her. She paid me no mind as she swooped her hair into two perfect buns on the top of her head.

I got out of the shower and dried off while Rose and Gardenia put on makeup and lip gloss, and boy, did they look pretty. I, on the other hand, looked like a wet dog! The more I brushed and blow-dried my hair, the more knotted and tangled it got.

"Help!" I yelled, but of course no one answered because they were too busy fixing themselves up. I wished Mom was here to help me get ready.

I grabbed one of Gardenia's hair ties from the drawer and tried to tie it around the tangled mop on the top of my head.

It didn't work! I was n-o-t NOT going onstage looking a mess.

Rose walked into the bathroom. She looked so beautiful. Her hair was shiny, her cheeks pink, and her lips glossy. I wanted to look just like her.

"What's wrong, Bean?" she asked.

"My hair's a mess and I'm gonna look ugly for the show."

"Let me help you."

Rose brushed and blow-dried my hair till it was a

pretty, fluffy poof. Then she tied a pretty pink bow around like a headband.

"Wanna wear some of my makeup?" she asked.

Was she kidding? Of course! I'd never really worn makeup before, except that time I played with Mom's lipstick and ended up looking like a clown. Rose softly brushed my cheeks with pink rouge and coated my lips with a sticky, sweet-smelling lip gloss. Just as she put the finishing touches on my face, Dad called from the hall, "Bean, Gabrielle and her mother are here!"

"Your hair looks great," Gabrielle said. She spun me around to get a better look. "Here is the dress, my very favorite one."

"I tried to talk her out of it." Gabrielle's mom shook her head. "But she was determined. You must be a good friend, Bean Gibson."

"Yes, we are very good friends," I said with a smile.

Gabrielle and I went into to my room. I took off my robe and climbed right into the ruffled pink-and-purple dress. Gabrielle zipped me up and tied the white sash in a big bow. I spun around in front of the mirror.

"You look so pretty!" Gabrielle said.

The door swung open. Rose, Dad, and Gabrielle's mom all piled in to get a glimpse.

"Wow!" Dad gasped.

"Now don't spill anything on that dress. It's very expensive," Gabrielle's mom said.

"Yes, ma'am."

"Don't worry, Ms. Davenport," said Dad. "Bean is very responsible."

Dad must not have remembered that time I climbed the tree behind the church in my best dress. I ripped it, got mud all over it, and got in big trouble. I'd take better care of Gabrielle's dress, though, I promised myself.

I took one more peek in the mirror before we headed out.

"Looking good," Gardenia said as she saw my reflection.

And I felt good too . . . pretty and confident and ready to perform.

17

Wiggly Legs and Shaky Hands

"See you there," I said to Gabrielle as she climbed into her mom's car.

"Break a leg," she said, and smiled.

I knew she didn't really want me to break a leg. That's just the way people say "Good luck" before a big performance.

Me and my sisters piled into Dad's car and we hit the road. I had butterflies in my tummy, but not bad ones. These butterflies were excited!

Gabrielle and her mom followed us to the college,

but when we got there, they disappeared because they had to park far away. Dad gets to park right up front in the teachers' lot. He has his very own parking spot with his name on it, you know.

We grabbed our instruments from the trunk and marched into the building. The walls were covered from ceiling to floor with holly and wreaths, and there was a huge Christmas tree right by the door. You could tell the holidays were almost here, for sure.

We followed the posters and signs that said HOLIDAY MUSICAL EXTRAVAGANZA to the auditorium, where people were beginning to arrive for the show. We walked down the aisle in the middle of the room, and as I passed row after row after row, those nervous butterflies chased the excited ones right out of my tummy. This place was h-u-g-e HUGE!

We climbed the stairs on the side of the stage and headed backstage. It was full of people getting ready for the show. I spotted Stanley putting his saxophone together.

"Hey, there!" I waved.

"Hi, Bean," Stanley said, and then turned his

attention back to his saxophone. I could see he was a little bit nervous too.

All the musicians were getting ready. Gardenia opened her flute case and started putting the shiny silver parts together. Rose sat down at the piano to practice her piece. A man with a beard was tuning his guitar, and a pretty lady was playing scales on a harp.

I got started prepping my violin too. I opened up the leather case and carefully pulled out the bow. It's very fragile, you know. I screwed the top gently to tighten the bow hairs, just like Dad had taught me, and rubbed the rosin up and down the strings to make them sticky and ready to play.

"Okay, we're going to start in a couple minutes," Dad announced to the performers. "We are going to perform tonight, youngest to oldest. Sorry, Jackson," Dad said with a wink at a man holding a trombone. He had gray hair, so I guessed he was the oldest.

Oh, wait! I looked around frantically, trying to find someone younger than me. No luck. I was the youngest—and that meant I was first.

"Dad," I said, "I can't play first."

"Sure you can, sweetheart. You're ready to go and looking good. You're the perfect start for tonight's performance."

"No way! I can't! I won't! I mean Mom isn't even here yet."

"Don't worry. She'll be here," Dad said, smiling to comfort me. Then he turned to Stanley. "You're up right after Bean."

"Please go before me," I begged Stanley.

"No way, Bean. Sorry," Stanley said, and I understood. Of course not! No one in their right mind would want to go first.

I peeked around the curtain, and when I saw the huge auditorium almost full to the brim with people, my legs got all shaky like noodles and I felt like I couldn't breathe.

Everyone was so busy tuning their instruments and warming up that they didn't notice when I ran down the hall and into the ladies' bathroom. I stared in the mirror and took a couple deep breaths. "You can do this," I said to myself. I stood up straight as an arrow, puffed out my chest full of deep courage-filled breaths, but then, as I turned to the door, I deflated like a balloon. It was no use. I was s-c-a-r-e-d SCARED!

I didn't know what else to do but hide until Mom got there . . . or the show was over. I ran into the last stall, locked the door, and sat on the seat with my legs crossed so no one could see me.

Someone came in to pee, and I closed my eyes and held my breath. Not a peep! Luckily, they flushed, washed their hands, and left without spotting me.

Then through the door, I heard Dad call in a muffled voice, "Five minutes, everyone!"

I held my breath, knowing that someone was gonna start looking for me.

"Bean? Are you in there?" Rose yelled as she peeked under the stall doors. She didn't see my feet, though, because I was curled up on the toilet seat.

The door shut behind Rose, and I let out a sigh of relief. Alone again . . . or so I thought.

"Bean!" Gardenia shouted, scaring me to death. She was standing on the seat in the stall next to mine, peering over. "Everyone is looking for you."

"I'm not going on, never!"

"Bean, it's gonna be okay. You've practiced and you're gonna be great," she said sweetly. Then she went back to her usual tone. "Now open the door and come out . . . now!"

Just as I opened the stall door, Gardenia grabbed my arm and dragged me out of the bathroom and back to the dressing room.

"What's wrong?" Rose said.

"I'm not going on. Mom's not here and she promised and I'm gonna mess up and . . . ," I whimpered as I fell into my sisters, who hugged me tightly. "Mom's never here when I need her."

"I know Mom gets stuck at work a lot, but we're here," Rose said.

"We love you. You're gonna be great!" Gardenia added.

I remember when I got in trouble with Tanisha and my sisters were worried about me. Even though my sisters love to torture me every chance they get, I know that when I really need them, they will always be there for me.

"Okay, everyone, it's time!" Dad called. "Bean, you're up."

"Dad, Bean really wants to wait for Mom to get here," Rose said.

"Do you think you could switch up the order?" Gardenia asked. "I don't mind going first."

"All right, I guess that would be okay," said Dad.

"Thanks," I said, and gave Gardenia a big hug.

"Welcome, everyone, to tonight's Holiday Musical Extravaganza with all our very talented local musicians," the announcer said. "Now put your hands together for our first performer and our youngest, Bean Gibson. Huh?" He was stopped short by a woman behind the curtain. They whispered for a minute, then he continued, "Okay. Change of plan. Please put your hands together for Gardenia Gibson on the flute."

I watched as Gardenia sashayed to the stage with her head held high. She is brave. Gardenia played a piece by Mozart so beautifully that I bet even he couldn't have played it any better. After her, a girl named Suzette played the guitar. She messed up a couple times, but the crowd didn't seem to mind.

Next, Stanley got onstage and played his jazz tune on his saxophone and everyone, including me, danced and clapped along. When he was done, the crowd went wild.

"You were awesome!" I told him, and gave him a big hug when he was done.

I was feeling a little more relaxed as I watched Rose play. She was amazing. She played Beethoven with both hands and without even one mess-up. The audience clapped and shouted.

"Okay, sweetheart, you're up," Dad whispered in my ear as Rose took her bow. "I know you are scared, but you're going to be great."

"But Mom's still not here," I whined. "And she promised."

"I know. I'm really sorry, sweetheart. I'm sad that she didn't make it too." Dad hugged me tight. "There are no more kids—and the show must go on."

My hands were shaking like earthquakes and my feet felt like sandbags stuck to the ground. I couldn't move, but Dad grabbed me by the arm and dragged me onstage.

With a kiss on the forehead, he said, "Go ahead, honey. Go play."

The curtain opened. I was frozen, with my violin and bow dangling at my sides. I looked out into the audience, and it was overflowing with strangers. They seemed like big, mean-looking men and creepy, strange-looking women—and they were all glaring at me. I wanted to turn and run, but my feet were superglued to the stage.

Slowly, I raised my violin to my shoulder and placed the bow on the strings. You can do this. You can do this, I repeated to myself. I took a huge believe-in-myself breath and pulled the bow to start. *Screeeeeeeeeech!*

Oh, no! *Screeeeeech!* I couldn't do it! *Screeeeeech!* I fought back the tears that were filling my eyes, but one got free and then they all started falling down my cheeks. They dripped down my chest onto Gabrielle's special dress, so now she was gonna be mad at me too. This was a disaster.

I turned and looked over my shoulder, and Stanley was waving. Rose, Gardenia, and Dad were there too. When I saw them all smiling back at me, it gave me a teensy tiny bit more courage. I took another deep breath and turned back to the audience.

The lights were just bright enough that, in the crowd of strangers, I spotted Carla and Sam, and there was Gabrielle too, and she didn't even look mad. I saw Tanya and Grand Mommy and Aunt Bobbie. The more I looked at the audience, the more familiar faces I saw and the better I started to feel.

I put my violin back on my shoulder and kept my eyes glued on all my friends. I started again and there was no screech. I played the whole song without another mess-up. When I was all done, everyone stood up and clapped for me.

I bowed and curtsied and bowed again and waved to all my friends.

When I came off the stage, Dad gave me the biggest bear hug ever and then took the stage with a few of his friends.

Dad played the guitar and sang while his friends

Jack and Tom played the drums and bass guitar. Rose joined them too and played the piano as they shook the house with what Dad calls "ol'-school rock." They were the hit of the show, for sure. Everyone got up and danced in the aisles. Gardenia grabbed my hand and we got onstage and danced too. Dad was beaming. This must be how he felt when he was in that band when he was young.

After the show, everyone met up backstage.

"How about we all go for ice cream?" Dad said cheerfully. "Tonight is a very special night."

"Yippee!" we all squealed, but then my happy face turned sour when I spotted Mom pushing through the crowd.

"I'm so sorry. I can't believe I missed it," she cried as she ran toward us with tears in her eyes. She knelt down in front of me and said, "I got a flat tire on the freeway, and it took forever to get someone to help me change it. Baby, I know I promised, but this time it was out of my hands."

Even though I'd made it through the performance alive, my body was still churning with angry and sad feelings. I could tell Mom felt bad, but this time I had really needed her and she had let me down . . . again.

I couldn't help the tears from filling up my eyes. My hands shook as I wiped my wet cheeks. I clenched my teeth and yelled, "You always miss everything!"

"I'm really, really sorry, Bean," Mom said, trying to console me.

But it was no use. My head was spinning from my fury. I opened my mouth again and screamed, "I hate you!"

Mom winced at my words, and all the people around us froze. I knew it was really mean to say, but I couldn't stop the fire burning inside.

"Bean, that's enough," Dad said sternly, but I spun around and ran away to get lost in the crowd.

"It's okay. Let her go," I heard Mom say to Dad as I left. She was crying. "She has every right to be upset."

I spotted Tanya first in the crowd that was still hanging out in the auditorium. I hadn't seen her in so long, and boy, had I missed her. I gave her a big hug, which made me feel a little better.

Just then, Carla ran up too and wrapped her arms around me. "You were awesome," she said.

"Thanks! I'm so glad you both were here. I don't think I would've been able to get through that without you guys."

"Hey, who's this?" Carla asked, motioning toward Tanya, who was standing next to me.

"Oh, meet my cousin and really great friend, Tanya. Tanya, this is my best friend, Carla."

"It's really cool to finally meet you. I've heard so much about you," Tanya said. "I'm glad everything worked out between you two."

"Yeah," said Carla. "We forgave each other."

"And now everything is great," I added, but my heart still felt like it was missing something, like Swiss cheese with all the holes. I felt bad about what I had said to Mom. I mean, of course, I don't hate her. I love her. I was just really, really mad, you know.

I guess we all make mistakes, though. I hadn't meant to be a bad friend to Carla, and she had forgiven me. My eyes flicked to Stanley in the crowd.

He had forgiven me for calling him names, and Gabrielle had too, for the muddy-water incident.

"I've been looking for you," Rose said, when she finally spotted me. "Everyone's waiting outside. Time to go."

"Wanna come for ice cream?" I asked Carla and Tanya.

"For sure!" they both cheered.

I grabbed Carla's hand with my right and Tanya's hand with my left as we headed out of the auditorium. We spotted Sam, Gabrielle, and Stanley and invited them too.

Mom, Dad, and the rest of the gang were waiting outside for us. I could tell Mom was still feeling really bad. Her eyes were red and her head was hanging low. Dad had his arm around her shoulder, trying to comfort her.

I ran up to Mom and grabbed her hand. "I'm sorry I made you sad, Mommy."

She hugged me tight and said, "I'm really sorry too, baby."

I wiped her tears from her cheeks and said, "It's

okay. Everyone messes up sometimes, and I know that, for sure, because I mess up a lot, you know. I don't want to be mad anymore."

"Oh, baby," Mom said as she hugged me tight. "You've become such a big girl and I am very proud of you. I love you so much."

"I love you more," I said as I snuggled deeper into her chest.

"I really wish I had been there to see you play."

Then I had a great idea. "Maybe I could play for you tonight when we get home?"

"That would be wonderful, baby," Mom said, finding her smile again.

It felt so much better to not be mad at Mom. I gave her one more hug, then went back to meet up with my friends.

We all ran down the block to Swirl Ice Cream Parlor. Stanley and Tanya got vanilla and chocolate swirled onto cones. Gabrielle got strawberry in a cup. Sam got a double scoop of pink bubblegum ice cream, and I ordered a double scoop of chocolate chunk and cookie dough in a waffle cone. Carla got the very same thing because it's our favorite.

Just as me and all my friends were about to pile around a picnic table outside, I spotted Tanisha kicking up dirt by the alley.

"Oh, no," Sam said. "Trouble's here."

Now I know Tanisha is a meanie and a bully, but something in my insides made me feel bad. I mean, she had no friends and no sisters and no ice cream. I got up.

"What are you doing?" Carla whispered, but I just kept walking.

"Umm . . . Tanisha," I said softly. "I was wondering if . . . um . . . you might wanna come join us."

"Why would I want to hang with you guys?" she said, still kicking dirt and staring at the ground. "Plus, I ain't got no money for ice cream."

"You could share mine," I said with a smile. Tanisha looked right at me, and—guess what? Her hard glare turned just a little softer, and without a word, she followed me to the table. I grabbed an extra spoon and we all dug into our creamy, cold, yummy ice creams.

I looked around the table and saw Tanya laughing with Carla and Gabrielle. Stanley and Sam sharing their ice cream and Tanisha . . . Well, she was shooting spitballs through a straw across the table at Stanley. Whatever!

I felt a happy feeling all over. It's funny, because while I was so busy whining about not having Carla and missing Tanya, I didn't realize that I had made so many good friends.

I smiled so big, my cheeks hurt. Then I licked my spoonful of ice cream.